About the

Alan Gorevan is an award-winning writer and intellectual property attorney. He lives in Dublin. Visit his website at www.alangorevan.com

By Alan Gorevan

NOVELS:
Out of Nowhere

NOVELLAS:
The Forbidden Room
The Hostage
Hit and Run

SHORT STORY COLLECTION:
Dark Tales

Dark Tales

Alan Gorevan

This book is a work of fiction. People, places, events and situations are the product of the author's imagination. Any resemblance to actual persons, living or dead, or historical events, is purely coincidental.

ISBN: 9798666298596

CONTENTS

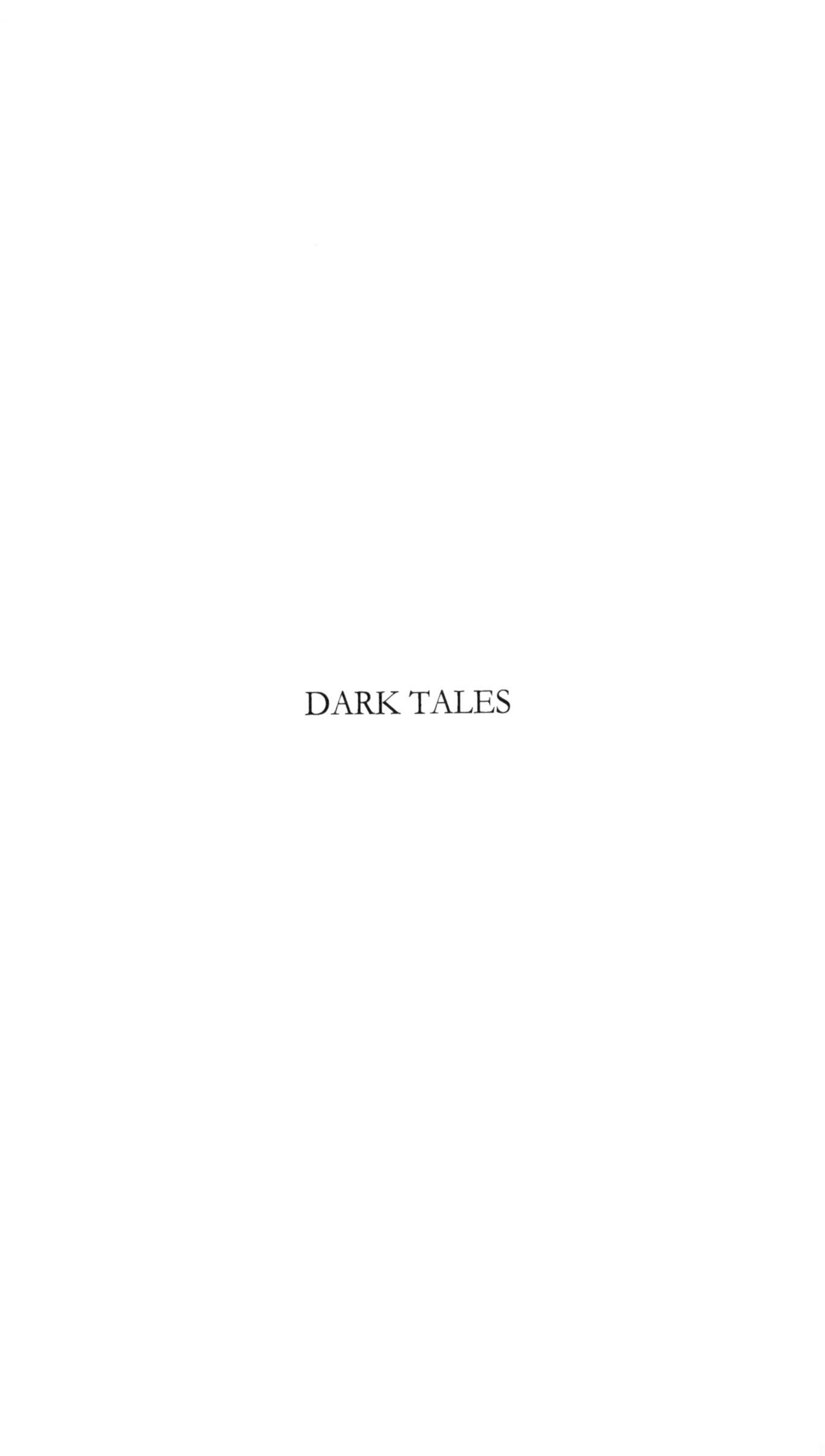

DARK TALES

While You Sleep

ONE

Light snowflakes filled the February air, falling slowly to the footpath. Tim Hennessy stepped out of Brixton Tube station. He paused next to a busker playing a saxophone, taking a moment to put his Oyster card back in his wallet.

Though he'd often taken the one-hour flight from Dublin, Tim had never been in London during a snow storm. Darkness had already fallen, but the sky glowed in the weird way of snowy days.

He was half an hour late, and he hoped he hadn't missed his Airbnb host, a graphic designer named Alex, who was meant to meet him at the apartment.

Tim checked the address on his phone, and set off walking down the street, dragging his cabin bag behind him, the virgin snow crunching under his boots. He stopped off at Sainsbury's on the way, to grab a sandwich and a Coke.

Cars eased along the road, moving only a little faster than Tim. Five minutes' walk took him to the address. The terraced brown-brick building had three storeys above the ground, but Tim's apartment was in the basement. He pushed open a creaking metal gate, and dragged his bag down the narrow steps.

His phone buzzed, but he paid it no attention. It was probably just Alex, checking where he was. No point stopping to read the message. Especially now that his fingers were numb from the cold.

At the bottom of the steps, Tim pressed the doorbell. He was pleased that the door looked new and solid. Next to it, a small window was protected by a crosshatch of metal bars. Secure, Tim thought.

Lights were on behind the curtains, so hopefully Alex hadn't given up on him yet.

Tim shuddered, partly from the cold, and partly from nerves. Even if he hadn't been in London for a horror movie festival, he might have been edgy. That was just his personality, though it was something Penelope never learned to like.

The door swung open.

Tim smiled at the lanky man standing in the doorway, long blond hair framing his pink face. He was about ten years older than Tim, maybe forty.

"Alex?" he said.

The man looked him up and down, stony-faced. "You must be Tim."

"Sorry I'm late," Tim said. "My flight was delayed by the weather."

Alex dismissed the apology with a wave of his hand. "You're here now. That's what matters. Come on in."

Tim stepped into the hall and waited for Alex to close the door. The place looked clean and modern, with varnished pine floors and warm terracotta paint on the walls.

"Do you mind taking off your boots?" Alex said.

"No problem."

Tim unlaced the boots and shrugged his feet out of them, then followed Alex to the sitting room. Alex slumped in one of the two big leather couches, gesturing for Tim to sit in the other.

Between the two men, flames blazed in the fireplace. Tim couldn't remember the last time he'd felt the warmth of an open fire. He'd forgotten the way the heat pressed against your face, how your eyes burned slightly from the coal. He gazed up at the vibrant oil paintings on the wall, prints of Van Gogh.

Alex sighed. "Well, you look normal enough."

"Pardon?"

"It's just that I've been letting this place out for two years now, and I've met some strange people."

Tim smiled. "I bet."

"Like the last guy. Creeped me right out. Always eating cough sweets. Never saw him without one. You should have seen how many wrappers he left in the trash."

Tim laughed.

"Well, I'm here for a horror movie festival. Horror fans are some of the nicest people you'll ever meet."

Alex said, "That's true, actually."

He gave Tim a quick run-down of the apartment, told him the Wi-Fi password and handed him the keys. He was out the door within five minutes.

Once he was alone, Tim walked around, taking a look at each room. A kitchen, two bedrooms, a sitting room, the hallway. He decided to take the larger bedroom. That one had a double bed, with identical bedside units and an identical wardrobe on each side.

Tim didn't bother unpacking. He just opened his cabin bag on the bedroom floor and took out a change of clothes. Alex had left him plenty of towels.

Nice guy, Tim thought.

He checked his phone. The text he had received earlier had been from Penelope. Tim had hoped she'd be able to get there tonight. She was coming on the train from Manchester. He glanced at her message and felt his heart sink.

Sorry. I won't make it tonight. Train cancelled because of storm. Hope to see you tomorrow.

Tim didn't reply. He would only be in London for two nights, and he figured he'd need all that time to patch things up with Penelope.

Oh well. Nothing he could do. Hopefully the trains would be back to normal tomorrow.

Tim showered. Afterwards, he slipped on a clean T-shirt and clean boxers, and brushed his teeth before slipping under the covers of the bed. It took a long time for him to fall asleep in the strange bedroom, despite his weariness – but finally he did nod off.

In the morning, Tim woke up disoriented. Everything looked strange, from the bed itself, to the lampshade on the ceiling to the twin wardrobes on either side of the bed.

It took him a moment to remember he was in Brixton.

He padded to the bathroom, still tired, and flicked on the light switch.

His eyes widened when he caught sight of himself in the bathroom mirror. Vicious pink scratches covered his face.

TWO

As Tim stared at himself in the mirror, his heart pounded, pounded so hard and so fast he was afraid it would tear through his chest.

He gripped the white ceramic of the sink and stared at his reflection in mute surprise. The bathroom was bitterly cold, making the hair on the back of his neck stand up.

Leaning close to the mirror, Tim examined his face. The biggest scratch started below his left eye and extended down to the corner of his mouth. It was narrow but bright pink. Another scratch stretched from the other corner of his mouth down to his chin. Smaller scratches appeared on his neck and forehead.

"How the hell did that happen?" he muttered.

Tim saw no blood – the skin wasn't broken – but he felt alarmed.

His bladder reminded him that he had come to the bathroom for a reason. He relieved himself, causing steam to rise in the frigid bathroom air.

Afterwards, he returned to the bedroom. He searched around under the pillows, wondering if something sharp had found its way into the bed and hurt him as he shifted his body during the night. A pin, perhaps? A sharp piece of plastic?

The search revealed nothing but two soft pillows, a soft duvet and a soft bedsheet. There was no sign of anything he could have scratched himself with.

Unless it was his fingernails. They were a little longer than he liked them to be.

Once Tim had dressed, he got his clippers out of his toilet bag. A small canvas bin sat in the corner of the bedroom, lined with a plastic bag. It was empty except for a receipt from a DIY shop.

CUTTING. £2.99.

"That would be a good name for a horror movie," Tim said.

He pulled the bin over to the bed, sat down in front of it and trimmed all his fingernails, aiming into the bin as he cut.

When he was finished, he checked his phone.

Nothing from Penelope.

Still early, he thought, though his phone said eleven thirty.

After tinkering with the central heating for a few minutes, and hopefully setting it to come on for the rest of the day, Tim headed out.

He planned to grab breakfast on the way to the cinema, before enjoying a day's worth of movies, back-to-back, with friends he hadn't seen in months. Some were Irish, others English. All were horror nuts. They met a couple of times a year, at events like

Fright Fest, Horrorthon, and other genre events. That was how he and Penelope had met.

Outside, the ground was white, though snow was no longer falling. The chill air made Tim's ears ache. He pulled up his hood and headed for the Underground station.

The day passed pleasantly. He met up with his friends and forgot about the scratches until someone asked about them. He shrugged off the question.

After the fifth and final movie of the day, he made his way back to Brixton on the Tube. Penelope had texted him while he was in the cinema.

More disruption today. See you tomorrow.

Tim sighed. His flight to Dublin the next afternoon was at three o'clock, so he wouldn't get to spend much time with Penelope, even if she reached London early.

He stopped off in Sainsbury's again and grabbed a microwave dinner on the way back to the apartment.

The apartment was cold, though Tim was sure he'd set the timer correctly. He tinkered with the settings again, and finally heard the heater clicking and clacking as it began to heat up.

He ate dinner at the kitchen table in silence, thinking about Penelope. Nothing would have pleased him more than to speak to her at that moment. He took out his phone and called her. The last time the two of them had spoken, she had said she was open to talking about things. Tim hoped she meant that.

A phone rang somewhere nearby. Tim didn't pay attention at first. He figured that the sound was coming from the apartment upstairs. But when he ended the call to Penelope, the ringing stopped at once.

Curious.

He dialled her number again and immediately heard a phone ringing somewhere nearby. Letting it ring, he followed the sound to the kitchen. When he was there, the sound seemed to be coming from the front of the building. He walked up the hall. A small telephone stand with a single drawer stood next to the door. Tim pulled the drawer open and found a phone inside. The screen was illuminated and said, "TIM CALLING".

Tim ended the call and stared at Penelope's phone.

She had come here? She had arrived? Then where was she? What about her text message?

He went back to the kitchen and checked the note Alex had left, which listed his phone number. It was already late, nearly ten o'clock, but Tim phoned Alex anyway. The host answered after two rings.

Tim said, "Sorry to bother you."

"No problem. Is everything ok with the apartment?"

"Yeah. It's just… you know the other person, my friend, who was meant to arrive yesterday?"

"The lady?"

"That's right. Did you hear anything from her?"

Alex said, "Yeah. She texted me yesterday and told me she'd be late."

"Nothing since then?"

"Sure. She arrived this afternoon. Haven't you seen her?"

"No," Tim said, his voice rising an octave. "You *met* Penelope?"

"Sure did. At about half four. I gave her the second key. She said she'd meet up with you later."

"I found her phone here, in the apartment, but I haven't seen her."

"Maybe she went out for something?"

"But why would she leave her phone here?"

Alex said, "I couldn't tell you. She arrived safe anyway. That's all I know."

It seemed that Alex wasn't able to clear up the confusion.

Tim said, "Okay. Thanks."

He waited up late, but Penelope never showed. Her text was so vague. *More disruption today. See you tomorrow.* The text never said she wasn't coming to London until tomorrow. She might have arrived but decided to stay with a friend. Or else she didn't want to see him after all. Tim didn't know what to think.

After midnight, his eyes began to droop, a cue that he ought to get some rest. He had a quick shower and went to bed.

He tossed and turned but couldn't settle. He thought of Penelope, then of the marks on his face.

"Stupid scratches," he muttered.

Could his fingernails really have caused those marks? He had never scratched himself before. If he was doing it now, what did that mean? Was it about stress?

An idea occurred to him.

He switched on the light and got his camera from his cabin bag.

He set the camera up on its tripod, on top of the bedside unit. He pointed it at the pillows and set it to video mode. The camera had plenty of storage space, so it ought to be able to record hours of video. Tim went back to bed. In the morning, if any more scratches appeared, he would know what had caused them.

Finally he lapsed into a fitful sleep.

THREE

During the night, Tim had a terrible nightmare.

He dreamed of daggers made of ice. Thousands of them were falling from a blood-red sky, each one lit up from within with an impossible, blinding light. In the dream, Tim was standing in a deserted field. Ice-daggers fell, stabbing him all over his body, sinking into his flesh and lighting up his insides.

He collapsed on his back on the frozen grass as the daggers stabbed him again and again. Looking up, he saw one immense dagger, much larger than the others, hurtle towards his face.

He screamed as it plunged into his eye.

Tim awoke in bed, drenched with sweat. It was morning. A pale light entered the room through the curtain on the barred window.

Brixton, he thought. *Movies.*

It was okay.

Just a dream.

He sat up, still giddy with fright, taking a moment to reassure himself. Then he lay back and closed his eyes while his breathing settled. He lay there for another half minute, until his bladder forced him out of the bed.

He went to the bathroom and relieved himself. His left eye ached, in the place where he had been injured in the nightmare.

Tim flushed the toilet and stepped over to the sink to wash his hands. He froze in front of the mirror.

He was scratched much worse than the previous morning, the pink lines criss-crossing his whole face, the marks deeper, angrier. The skin was broken in many places, but it was his eye that made Tim stare in horror – or rather the eyelid.

Blood dripped from it.

He pressed the eyelid down with one hand and stared at his reflection with the other eye. His eyelid was crusted with almost-dry blood. It had been stabbed, Tim thought. He could see small, round marks. The sight of the injury made Tim's blood turn cold, like the daggers in his dream.

A shiver of fear raced through his body, travelling down his legs to his feet.

He hurried out of the bathroom and walked around the apartment. Nothing else seemed amiss. Penelope's phone sat where he had left it, on top of the stand in the hall. There was no sign of Penelope herself.

Tim returned to the bedroom. He felt the pillows again, squeezing them, running his hands over them, seeing if he had missed something sharp during his search the previous day. Again, he found nothing.

The injury was no accident, and he hadn't done it to himself.

Or had he?

How could he be certain?

Tim checked his own phone. He had received a message from Penelope during the night.

I'm here, baby.

Tim's hands became clammy. He wiped the cold sweat off the screen of his phone, and read the message again.

Here? Where was *here*?

How could she have texted him when he had both phones?

The sudden urge to get away, to run, overpowered him, but he fought back the feeling.

He remembered the camera. Hopefully it had caught everything, whatever weird thing was happening. He went and got the camera from the bedroom, and set it down on the kitchen table. It was still recording. He stopped it.

Standing at the table, he began to play the video from the start. He saw himself getting into bed, saw his restless tossing and turning. The recording was dark, but he could make out his own form under the covers, his head sticking out.

He skipped ahead an hour, then another couple of hours. His head turned this way and that, his body shifted about. There was still nothing to see – no sign of any injury or anything that might cause one.

He skipped ahead to near the end of the recording – and found something.

A dark form walked into view. Tim couldn't tell if they were a man or a woman, only that the person seemed to be thin and tall, and wore a dark cape with a hood.

Tim was vaguely aware of his mouth falling open.

Transfixed by the sight of the dark figure, he watched the video as it continued playing. The figure leaned over Tim's sleeping form. Tim was lying flat on his back, facing the ceiling.

The figure reached a thin arm out towards him, something small and pointy held between their fingers.

Tim leaned forward, trying to see what the object was.

He would have been willing to bet that it was a toothpick.

Slowly, as if enjoying it, the figure began running the toothpick over Tim's face, drawing it from mouth to cheek, across the neck, around the bottom of the nostrils – scratching, scratching, scratching. The movement became harder, more forceful. Then Tim saw himself shift in the bed. His mouth twitched. That might have been when he was dreaming of the ice.

The blazing ice-daggers.

Tim's movement seemed to anger the figure, and they jabbed Tim in the cheek with the toothpick. Then they hovered their hand over Tim's eye, and stabbed him there. They brought the toothpick down again, as if trying to pierce the eyelid and stab right through it to the eyeball.

Tim could hardly stifle the nausea sweeping up his throat.

Even though he was watching a recording of what had already happened, he could not help dreading what was to come.

The figure now held the toothpick stuck into Tim's eyelid, and ground the point of it down and around in a circle.

Tim grabbed his phone.

He needed to summon the police immediately. He dialled 999 and listened to the start of the recorded message. While he waited to talk to an operator, Tim continued watching the video.

In the video, he shifted in bed. He must have been waking up, which wasn't surprising, given the attack he'd suffered.

The mysterious figure glided away from the bed. They opened the door of the wardrobe beside the bed and stepped inside.

The phone dropped from Tim's hand.

He heard the operator, a pleasant-sounding lady, asking what his emergency was, but Tim couldn't speak.

He kept watching the video, which showed him sit up in bed, then lie back down again.

Tim realised that this part of the recording was from only a few minutes ago.

The mysterious figure, the shadowy form which had tried to gouge Tim's eye out, must still be in the bedroom, just feet away from him.

FOUR

Tim armed himself with a knife from the drawer. A long steak knife with a sharp-looking blade. He tested the point on his own finger. His hands were shaking so much that he cut himself, making a bright-red bubble of blood appear.

Well, the knife was sharp enough.

Children walked past on the footpath outside, laughing and shouting. Tim couldn't see them, only heard their cheerful voices, which sounded like something from another world. Tim's ears were filled with the throbbing of his own blood, pumping like crazy.

He made his way over to the wardrobe.

Wiping his right hand on his T-shirt, Tim gripped the knife again. He held it up, ready to strike. With his left hand, he reached for the wardrobe's doorknob.

He took a breath – and pulled the door open.

Nothing jumped out at him. No shadowy figure with toothpicks. Instead, a young woman sat inside the wardrobe. She wore a jacket, jeans and boots. Her eyes were closed and her wrists were bound together.

"Penelope?"

The knife fell from his hands, hitting the floor with an awful *clang*.

Tim didn't need to touch her to confirm that she was dead, but he crouched down and pressed his hand to her cheek. It was cold. Her head was tilted towards the back of the wardrobe. Tim was glad of that, at least. He didn't want to see her face.

Tears rolled down his cheeks, stinging him as the salty tears seeped into his wounds.

Penelope must have been dead for hours, possibly even for a day.

Where was the shadowy figure? Penelope certainly wasn't the person he had seen in the video. But that person had stepped in here.

Or had they?

"Wait," Tim whispered.

He realised that the camera had not been pointed towards this wardrobe. It had been pointed towards the identical one on the other side of the bed. In his panic, Tim had forgotten that both sides of the room looked the same.

Slowly, Tim got to his feet.

He could hear movement behind him. The gentle sound of fabric passing through the air. One light footstep, then another. Tim tensed, his senses heightened.

The clicking sound of teeth on something hard. The scent of lozenges on the air.

Tim swallowed.

He saw a dark form in the corner of his eye. As he turned, something hard hit his face and darkness swept over him.

FIVE

The next day was warmer, and the snow was half-melted by noon, when Alex made his way to the basement apartment. He was about to press the doorbell when he caught sight of an envelope on the ground.

ALEX was scrawled across the front of it in black marker.

He bent down and picked it up. The two keys to the apartment were inside. The horror guy, Tim, must have left already.

Alex stifled his irritation. Someone besides him could have seen the envelope there and taken the keys, though he supposed that wasn't likely.

Alex let himself in and walked around the apartment, flicking on the lights as he checked each room. The place was in good shape. No serious cleaning needed, which was a relief as Alex only had an hour until his next guests arrived. That booking was for a Danish couple and their daughter.

He set about changing the bedclothes and setting out fresh towels.

He wondered what was going on between Tim and Penelope. They seemed like nice kids. Alex hoped they sorted things out. They'd be cute together.

When he was emptying the bin bag in the bedroom, he saw that there were dozens of lozenge wrappers in there.

"Huh," Alex said. It reminded him of…

He shrugged. Maybe Tim had caught a cold.

A receipt at the bottom of the bag caught his attention, because it was from the hardware shop down the road. He wondered what business any of his guests had going there.

CUTTING. £2.99.

"Unbelievable."

Alex snorted in disbelief. What kind of jerk thought it was okay to get a copy of Alex's key cut?

Not cool, horror guy.

Now Alex would have to go and change the lock, and that would eat into his profit margin.

He was wondering how much it would cost when the doorbell rang.

An hour had passed quickly. Alex gathered up the bin bag and brought it to the kitchen where he emptied it into the larger bin.

He decided he'd change the lock in three days, when the Danes had gone. He didn't want to disturb them during their stay.

Rivals

Dennis Geary, the man the world knew as "the Biscuit Baron" was still in high spirits when his limo approached the gates of his Dalkey home.

"That was the best goddamned funeral I've ever been at," he said. "Bar none."

His wife, Miriam, slapped his arm. "Dennis, don't say that."

"Jesus Christ, remember when that priest forgot the name of Bob's son? I just about shit myself laughing."

Dennis ran a hand through his grey hair and gave Miriam a wolfish grin.

Miriam said. "Do you have to be so… so *crude*? With your *damn this* and *damn that*?"

"I'm American. What do you expect?" He said it as if he hadn't lived in Dublin for the last twenty years.

Miriam rolled her eyes. "You're fifty percent American and fifty percent Irish."

"Whatever. I'm one hundred percent alive, which is more than you can say for Bob."

Miriam's mouth dropped open. "Dennis."

"Sweetheart, you know I'm just speaking my mind."

"Yes, well…"

She gazed out the window. Not much was visible through the rain. The sky was dark, as if it was late evening rather than the middle of the afternoon.

Dennis patted Miriam's leg. She was still the right side of forty, but so old-fashioned, you'd have sworn she was born during WW2. Dennis would have left her if he didn't think the divorce would be such a bitch.

He pulled the Champagne out of its ice bucket and topped up his glass. Miriam hadn't touched hers, but he added a couple of drops anyway, just so she couldn't call him stingy.

It had been raining at the graveyard, turning to sleet near the end of the ceremony. Dennis had got a little wet, even with his driver holding an umbrella over him, but he didn't mind. It was worth it to see Bob getting lowered into the dirt.

The steel-framed PVC gates of the house came into view. Their driver pressed a button and the gates slowly started to open. Normally the tedious wait annoyed Dennis, but not today. He unrolled his copy of the *Irish Tribune* and opened it at the page-nine tribute to Bob.

Page nine.

Dennis grinned.

Seeing Bob's obituary brought it home to Dennis that he was really gone. It made the fact real. On the

the rest of the day, so all my employees can celebrate too?"

"I don't think that would be very nice," Miriam said.

Dennis was surprised to see tears in her eyes. "What's wrong, sweetheart?"

The driver got out and walked around to Miriam's side. He opened the door and waited for her to get out.

"Give us a minute," Dennis barked. "Shut the damn door."

The driver did.

Miriam found a tissue in her handbag and dabbed her eyes.

She said, "I'm sorry. I just wish people could be a little kinder to each other. Life isn't all about money."

You married a millionaire, Dennis thought. She didn't do it for the money, he was sure, but the end result was the same. He said, "I know, sweetheart."

"I want Kim to grow up knowing the value of kindness."

"She will. Our girl will grow up right. I promise."

And he really meant it. Kim was the only person in the world that he really loved, his perfect princess.

Dennis squeezed Miriam's knee. She was right about the factory. Shutting down production was a bad idea. It would just be a waste of money. Not that money was all Dennis cared about. He wasn't miserly the way people said. He believed in quality too. His company's biscuits were made using the finest flour, for example, and the flavouring was almost entirely natural.

Dennis hadn't skimped on the hitman either.

The guy he hired wasn't cheap, but he'd done a great job, and that was what mattered. The coroner was satisfied Bob had died of natural causes.

However, Dennis had seen the way Bob Junior looked at him in the graveyard. Hate. Loathing. Suspicion. And something else Dennis hadn't yet pinned down. He almost thought he'd seen the little bastard leer.

Dennis realised the driver was still standing outside in the rain.

"Let's go inside," he said, and reached past Miriam to bang his fist on the window. The driver opened the door at once.

They hurried into the house. It was warm and bright inside.

Sophia, the housekeeper, bowed to them as they entered.

"Where's Kim?" Dennis asked.

"In her room all day."

Dennis made his way upstairs and walked down the hall to Kim's room. He opened her door without knocking.

"Sweetheart?"

The window was open and the curtains were billowing in the wind. Kim's room looked out onto a leafy section of the garden at the side of the house. A fire-escape led from the window to the ground below. Dennis leaned out the window and looked down, in case Kim might have gone outside for some reason, but there was no sign of her.

Dennis straightened up and closed the window.

He caught sight of a A4 sheet of paper on Kim's bed. Something was scrawled on it in red marker. Dennis picked the sheet up and read it.

Then he read it a second time, with tears in his eyes.

Soon he was crying out loud, huge sobs shaking his body. He heard Miriam coming rushing but he couldn't pull himself together. Couldn't put on a brave face this time. Instead he read the note again.

She's gone. Now we're even, it said.

Dead End

ONE

The area around Riverside Business Park was deserted at seven in the morning. Many businesses had closed down and the place had an eerie feel, especially on a dark February day.

Denise O'Brien jogged along the perimeter footpath, moving at an easy pace, past a closed-down car dealership, then a closed-down plumbing supplies shop. The shop's window was broken and the area outside was littered with cider cans, dirty clothes and the remnants of a fire. The fire must have been burning the previous night – Denise detected the faint smell of smoke.

Her ears were numb from the cold. She would have liked to be at home, under the duvet with her boyfriend, James, to keep her warm. But she had set herself a task, and once she did that, she finished it.

That meant running every day until she achieved her goal.

Most joggers avoided this part of Dublin since the attacks, but Denise had been running in the area for two months and had experienced nothing more than boredom and a slightly elevated pulse.

She coughed as she turned a corner, down the side of the industrial estate. The sound cut through the silent air.

She came across two tents, where homeless people had set up camp. A makeshift laundry line was strung between two buildings.

Denise's mother blamed homeless people for the attacks. Denise didn't contradict her. She also didn't tell her mother where she went for her morning run. They came from a long line of stubborn women, and Denise didn't want an argument.

She passed the tents without incident and came to a turn. She set off down the road that ran through the middle of the business park. The road was wide, and the footpaths were lined by dead grass. Most of the buildings were three or four storeys tall, decades old and aging badly.

Her running shoes slapped the footpath at a steady pace. James had asked her why she took up jogging. She was already in great shape, and she spent so much time working.

It was true that she swam every Saturday morning and hit the gym three times a week.

James was sweet, but lazy.

He just wanted her to stay in bed and fool around with him. Denise had a determination James lacked, a resolve to do what was needed.

Denise pushed herself to run harder. She still wasn't sweating despite the padded vest she wore.

Light gloves protected her hands from the cold. Without them she would have lost feeling in her fingers, it was so cold. It was bad enough that her ears ached.

When she came to an unfamiliar turn, she took it, curious to see where the road would lead.

The offices were smaller here, only lining one side of the road. A tall wall stood on the other side. Denise looked up at the sky, noticing that it was starting to brighten. Somewhere, birds began to sing.

She followed the road to a dead end, where a half-built office stood. The construction site was surrounded by a metal fence with a big hole in it. It looked like the project had been abandoned. A graffitied hut for workers stood behind the fence.

Denise stopped, took a breath and stretched. She turned, ready to go back the way she had come.

That was when the man appeared out of nowhere, right in her face, a huge form in a puffy black jacket, his head shaved, his eyes small and dark, like a pig's, but set deep in an enormous pink face. His fist was enormous too, and it smashed into Denise's face.

A moment of surprise, and Denise crumpled to the ground.

TWO

Denise's head bounced off the footpath. She was dazed for a moment but she shook off the feeling and scrambled to her feet.

The man came up behind her. Before she could escape, a huge arm hooked around her throat and got her in a headlock. The man dragged her backwards like that, her feet kicking out helplessly, her hands clawing to break free.

He pulled her tight against him. Even through the padding of his jacket, she could feel the powerful muscles in his arm, and the hardness of his chest.

"Don't struggle or I'll make it ten times worse," he said. "I promise you that. I'll cut off your hands."

His breath stank of cigarettes but his voice was a high-pitched squeak, at odds with his rough look. For some reason, his conversational tone chilled her more than anything else.

He dragged Denise to the hole in the fence. She tried to call out, but with his arm clamped around her throat, she could barely even breathe, let alone shout. The roughly cut metal scratched her face as the man pulled her through to the other side. She heard him open the door of the construction workers' hut.

The man released her from the headlock.

He shoved her inside the hut.

Denise fell on the floor in the corner. She turned and looked around her. The hut was dark and almost empty. The only furniture was a folding chair and a small table on the other side of the room. The hut had one window, but she'd never manage to fit through it, even if she could get it open. The place stank of urine.

She wondered how long the man had been here, whether he had used this place before.

For other women.

"I'm glad you came back," he said. "I saw you jogging yesterday and I thought, *she's a good one*. That haughty way of running. You hold your head up so high. Or you used to. Not now."

The man smiled, revealed two rows of crooked, yellow teeth.

Denise felt a flash of anger. She always prided herself on her observation skills, but she hadn't clocked him watching her. And he was big enough to notice. He stood well over six feet tall and must have weighed more than two hundred pounds. She would have estimated his age at forty.

She got to her feet, pushing herself up off the rough floor with both hands.

When the man flicked a switch, a fluorescent bulb overhead flickered into life, blinding Denise. Once her eyes adjusted, she caught sight of a set of knives in a canvas case. It lay open on the table, revealing an array of brutal blades, all gleaming in the light. The man ran his fingers lovingly along them.

"Let's start small," he said, resting his fingers a serrated blade, about three inches long. "With the ears," he added.

A chill ran down Denise's neck.

It was impossible to get out of the hut without going through the man. He was blocking the only exit.

He pulled the knife out of its case. He turned with a smirk on his face and took a step towards her. Denise tried to back away, but her backside pressed against the wall. She had nowhere to go.

In a second he had crossed the room.

He said, "Don't fight. Don't scream. Follow my instructions and I'll let you live."

He stepped closer, tossing the knife from his right hand to his left.

Denise had read reports of the attacks. She could even remember the victims' names: Deirdre Gallagher and Vivian Smith. Both women were alive, if you could call it that. As far as Denise knew, their lives would never be normal again.

The man took another step closer.

With a speed that belied his size, he reached out with his free hand and swatted her in the face. The blow knocked her head to the side.

He said, "I like a little boxing before getting into the wet work."

Denise had only straightened up when another blow rocked her head to the other side. She reached out and grabbed the wall to stop herself from falling.

She felt dizzy, as if her brain was sloshing around inside her head.

The end of a length of electrical cable stuck out of his pocket. He had used the same stuff to tie up the other victims, before raping and mutilating them. He began to pull the cable out of his pocket, clearly enjoying her dread.

She said, "Philip, wait."

The man glared at her.

"What did you say?"

"It *is* Philip, isn't it? Philip O'Connell?"

"How do you know my name?" he growled.

THREE

"I asked you a question," Philip O'Connell said, stepping closer. His face turned a furious purple and a vein bulged in the middle of his forehead.

Of course he was furious. His whole aim was to take control, and Denise had just gone and clawed some of it back.

But she couldn't help feeling intimidated as he towered over her, twice her size.

She thought of what the victims had said initially, before they decided it was prudent to stop talking about the attacks. Deirdre Gallagher had spoken of how big the guy was, how strong. Vivian Smith had talked about the psychological torture of his threats during her six-hour ordeal. Both women reported feeling helpless.

Denise felt some of that too, as Philip rushed at her.

He grabbed her by the throat and pushed her against the wall. As he squeezed the life out of her,

Denise found it impossible to think of anything except getting his hands off her.

He said, "How do you know my name?"

Denise gasped. She couldn't have answered if she wanted to.

Her lungs burned from the lack of oxygen. Her mind became fuzzy.

She was about to pass out.

Then Philip released his grip.

He stared at her as she slumped to the dirty floor.

She opened her mouth to speak when Philip unleashed a volley of kicks. She shielded her head as best she could, but each blow unleashed an explosion of shock and pain within her. His heavy boot hit her arms, elbows, legs… Maybe the attack only lasted half a minute, but it felt like forever.

He was breathing hard when he finished.

Denise watched as he turned away from her and walked to the other end of the hut.

"It's tough luck you know who I am. I can't let you go. But we can have some fun before you die."

He looked down at his array of weapons, taking his time to select a different one.

Denise didn't give him a chance.

She had a surprise of her own.

She pulled the switchblade out of her padded waistcoat. Philip cocked his head at the click of the knife opening, but Denise was already right behind him by then. When he whipped around, she plunged the knife into his chest, aiming for the heart.

Colleagues complained that Denise was a perfectionist, but she thought it was worth doing things right.

Philip stared at her. For a second, she feared that the blade was too short to penetrate Philip's chest and reach his heart, even though she had hit him in the right spot. But after a moment, he slumped to the floor.

"How did you know my name?" he rasped.

His last words.

Denise didn't answer.

When she was sure he was dead, she stepped out of the hut.

Her car was parked half a mile away, in the usual place. She jogged to it, got inside and drove it back to the business park, parking near the construction hut. She had matches in the glove compartment and a jerrycan full of petrol in the boot.

She thought Philip O'Connell would burn well.

He did.

FOUR

At home, Denise went straight into the shower. She spent a little longer than normal under the hot water, taking her time as she soaped her whole body and let the hot water ease her aching muscles. She took the chance to wash her hair too, as she liked to leave the house feeling completely clean. She'd have bruises soon, but that was okay. She'd think of an excuse.

After she'd finished in the shower, she went to the bedroom with a towel cinched around her waist.

James was stirring.

He said, "Good morning, beautiful."

"Morning."

"You went running already?"

"Sure." She ignored his open arms, inviting her back to bed. "I have to get to work," she said.

"You work too much."

"We had a busy patch. I think things are going to quiet down soon."

"Yeah, right."

"Really," she said. "Maybe you and I can take weekend break soon. You know, Paris, Milan, something like that."

She walked over to the bed and gave him a kiss, before putting on her suit and a fresh shirt.

Denise had a couple of boiled eggs with an avocado for breakfast, then drove to the station. She arrived ten minutes before her shift was due to start. The sky was bright now, and a cool blue.

Detective Sergeant Ian Callaghan stood outside the station, smoking. Ian's face was sullen and he smoked his cigarette like it had insulted him.

Denise stepped out of the car and walked over.

"Bad news?" she said.

"On the O'Connell case. The second victim, Vivian Smith? Last night she rang. It turns out she's suddenly come down with a case of amnesia. She can't be sure it was Philip O'Connell that attacked her."

"As we expected. He got to her."

"We let him."

Ian always took these things so personally. Denise did too, but she figured she handled it better.

Ian scowled.

He said, "I hate seeing scumbags like Philip O'Connell get away with it. They think they can intimidate *anyone*. Talk about adding insult to injury. The things he did to those women. Then he comes along and threatens them. Sometimes I feel like… I just wish I could…"

He shook his head in frustration.

"Don't be stupid," Denise said. "We can only do our job."

"I know. But bastards like him are going to do it again and again. They don't change. You know that."

Denise heard a siren in the distance. She thought of the body burning in construction hut, and wondered if the fire had been reported yet.

She said, "Who knows, Ian? We might catch a break."

He snorted. "When has that ever happened?"

"I know what will make you feel better. Let's get a coffee."

"Finally, a sensible idea."

Denise smiled.

Ian would be so pleased when he found out about Philip O'Connell.

And James would be glad when she told him she didn't need to go jogging in the mornings anymore. The gym and the pool really were enough to keep her in shape.

The Message

ONE

It started with a newspaper.

I opened the front door on Monday morning and found one sitting on the doorstep, wrapped in plastic. I stepped outside. The July sky was clear. The only sound came from birds chirping in the trees. It was just half seven, so whoever delivered the paper had done their rounds early.

I picked the paper up and walked down the driveway so I could see past the hedge that enclosed our garden. Already, I could feel a little warmth from the sun on my bare arms.

Lia called from the bedroom window. “What are you doing, Keith?”

I couldn’t see anyone, so I went back inside.

“Some kid delivered a paper to the wrong house.”

Lia met me in the hallway, coming down the stairs in an exaggerated runway style. I remembered that she had a photoshoot today. She was looking as lovely as ever. Her chestnut hair was straight as a ruler. She was in jeans and a red blouse, tied above the belly button to show her taut stomach.

"That's weird," Lia said. "I wonder who it belongs to."

I shrugged. "Your guess is as good as mine."

We rarely bought a newspaper, though I preferred a paper copy to reading articles on my phone. And Lia was a huge crossword fan, so I figured she wasn't going to object to keeping the paper.

I brought it into the kitchen, noticing that the plastic wrap was already torn. Lia wrapped her slim arms around my waist as I ripped it open fully. That day's edition of *The Irish Times* fell onto the table.

A loose sheet of A4 paper slipped free and hit the floor. Lia picked it up. One side was plain white. The other side had huge black letters scrawled across it.

I'M PREGNANT.

"What the hell?" Lia said with a laugh. "Is that an ad?"

I looked at the page.

"I don't think so. It's not printed, it's written by hand. Maybe someone slipped it into the plastic with the paper."

She gave me a look. "What does it mean?"

"I don't know."

She stared at it. "It's so weird."

I said, "Maybe it wasn't meant for us. Or else someone is messing with us. Anyway, I better get to work."

Jack, our British Longhair, came through the cat flap with a *meow*. He turned his peach-flesh eyes on me.

"I'll give Jack some milk," Lia said. "You go to work."

She kissed me goodbye and dropped the page into the bin.

TWO

I woke early on Tuesday, maybe because I was so hot. I'd taken off my T-shirt during the night. Early for me was six in the morning. Lia and I had left the bedroom window open overnight. Now the net curtain swayed in the breeze. I watched it move for a minute before I swung my legs over the side of the bed.

Lia was still sound asleep, so I moved as quietly as I could while I got dressed and padded downstairs. I got the coffee going and ate an overripe banana with a yoghurt. Our bananas always seemed to go from hard and green to smelly mush without anything in between. I mused on how that could be possible while I looked out the window. Our washing hung on the line strung across the garden. While I waited for the coffee to be ready, I brought the clothes inside. They were all bone dry.

Yesterday's copy of *The Irish Times* sat on the table, open on the crossword page. Lia had filled in almost all of the answers. I expected nothing less. She was good at puzzles. I poured myself a coffee and scanned the page for any clues she hadn't got.

Actually, there was only one word.

With child. Eight letters.

_ R E _ N A _ _

I felt the skin on my cheeks prickle.

It was such a strange coincidence. Or was it?

The paper felt dry in my hands as I brought the crossword closer to my face and stared at it.

Lia hadn't said anything about this clue, but she'd still been doing the crossword when I went to bed. After six months of marriage, we hadn't yet managed to synchronise our sleep schedules. Normally I hit the sack first and she joined me later.

I threw the paper down on the table. I tried to push it out of my mind too, as I went to the bathroom to brush my teeth.

At half seven, I was ready to leave for work. I grabbed my keys and opened the door.

I nearly kicked over the milk bottle on the doorstep.

I hadn't even seen a milk bottle in about thirty years. Did people still get milk delivered? I thought that went out of fashion a long time ago.

I stared down at the bottle. The birds had got at it already. Its foil lid was pierced.

"What's up?"

The voice startled me. I spun around to see Lia's sleepy face. Her hair cascaded around her shoulders. She was still in her pink PJs. Her fans would have been amused to see the famous model dressed so casually.

"You scared the hell out of me."

She laughed and came over. We both looked down at the bottle.

"Oh my god. There's another weird item on our doorstep?"

I nodded. "We can't even drink it. Not after the birds got at it. Do you know anyone around here who gets milk delivered? Maybe some of the older people?"

"No," Lia said. "Does it have a label or anything?"

I bent down and picked the bottle up. The side facing me had nothing on it. I rotated the bottle. A white label was stuck on the other side.

I'M PREGNANT, was written on it in black marker.

Lia swallowed.

"Should we be scared?" she said.

THREE

Over dinner on Tuesday evening, Lia kept asking me what the messages were about, as if I knew. I could feel her eyes boring into me as she ate her salad. My mouth was so dry, I could hardly even swallow.

She said, "Come on, Keith. The note in the paper, the crossword clue, the milk bottle. Someone's trying to send you a message and they're not being subtle about it. If you're seeing someone else…"

I may have raised my voice.

Okay, I might have shouted.

"I don't know any more than you. They've got the wrong guy."

I could see she didn't believe me. But she said, "I hope so."

"You think I'm cheating on you?"

Which earned me a shrug.

Not exactly a vote of confidence. I couldn't believe her. I decided to stay up and see if another delivery came.

At midnight, I turned off the lights in the sitting room and left the curtains open. I even left the floor-to-ceiling window ajar so I'd hear it if someone walked up the driveway. I sat there, with only a dim lamp lit, ready to pounce on anyone who approached the house.

There wasn't much to see. The hedge around our front garden shielded most of the road outside from view. A couple of people walked past. I got a brief glimpse and then they were gone.

No one came up the driveway.

Jack appeared briefly, purring and looking to be rubbed. After checking in with me, he went out the cat flap again.

Lia stayed up till 2 am. She sat in the dining room reviewing photos from her last shoot and drafting an e-mail to her agent.

I kissed her goodnight before she went to bed.

"Join me," she said.

I would have liked to, but I stayed where I was and continued staring out the window. After a few minutes, my eyes began to feel heavy.

The birds woke me with their chirping at seven fifteen on Wednesday morning.

It was a late start for me, but I still felt exhausted. I was still on the couch. I'd failed as a guard, falling asleep on the job. My (mostly) sleepless night had been a waste of time.

When I sat up, a sheet of paper tumbled off my chest and onto the floor. I felt a stab of horror as I picked up the page.

Blank on one side. The other side said, *I'M PREGNANT.*

FOUR

All day Wednesday, I was furious. Mostly at myself. The previous night I'd left the window open so I could hear any intruder approach. In fact, I'd fallen asleep and someone had come in through the window and left a note right on my chest.

I couldn't stop thinking about that.

What kind of person did such a thing?

I searched the house, but found no sign of any other interference. No more notes. And the intruder was certainly gone. They hadn't hung around.

I woke Lia and told her what had happened. I wanted her to be especially vigilant, though she would be out at a shoot all day.

Lia's expression, when I told her, was hard to read. It contained suspicion, for sure. And fear too.

"I'm freaked out, Keith."

"So am I."

She said, "You're sure you heard nothing? You saw *nothing*?"

"No." I cleared my throat. "I… uh… I fell asleep."

"Good job," she said.

There was no time to complain about her sarcasm. Back downstairs, I scrambled to eat a mushy banana, nearly choked on a yoghurt and gave my teeth the most pathetic brushing they'd had in years.

All day at work, I thought about the messages. They were insane. Demented. Only a crazy person would try to communicate in such a way. I wished the messages would give more information, so I could figure out who they were really intended for, because there was no chance in hell they were meant for me.

After dinner, I told Lia, "I'm going to stay up again tonight."

"What do you mean, *again*? As I recall, you didn't stay up last night."

I let that one go and made myself a pot of strong coffee.

"Do you want to wait up with me tonight?" I asked.

Lia shook her head.

"I have another shoot tomorrow. Panda eyes don't look good on camera."

"Right. How was today's shoot?"

She cocked an eyebrow. "Oh, you finally remembered I had one?"

"Lia—"

"Don't pretend you care. If my career ended, you'd probably be glad."

"What? Do you really think that's fair?"

I wanted to say more, to tell her it wasn't true. But she was walking up the stairs before I could gather my thoughts.

And maybe there was a sliver of truth in it.

Whenever I saw Lia modelling a swimsuit or a bracelet or whatever, part of me was proud of her for rising to the top of her profession. But another part of me felt a stab of unease. Especially when she did a shoot with a male model.

Sometimes they pretended to be a couple. Sometimes they embraced.

Yeah, I hated that.

But Lia was great at what she did. She had that poise. That finesse. And I knew that being a model had been her dream since she was a kid. There was no way she was going to give it up for any reason.

I was thinking all this as I sat on the couch, cradling my coffee. A baseball bat lay next to me. So did my phone, in case I wanted to take a photo of the intruder, or call for help.

I was determined to stay awake this time.

And I did.

I read a mystery novel by the light of a lamp. I kept stealing glances out the window, but there was no one there.

Nothing to see.

When morning came, I felt deflated.

I brought my mug of cold coffee into the kitchen. While I was rinsing it in the sink, I glanced out the window to the back garden.

A T-shirt I didn't recognise hung from the line. It was white, with text scrawled across the chest in black marker.

I'M PREGNANT, it read.

FIVE

I called in sick at work so that I could stay home. Understandably, Lia was freaked out when she saw the T-shirt on the line.

"This is crazy," she said. "You saw nothing?"

I shook my head. Whoever it was that entered our back garden, they must have snuck around the side of the house when I wasn't looking. It would have been easy to do. We had a gate at the side of the house, but there was no lock. All you had to do was turn the handle and the gate opened.

"We need to call someone," Lia said. "I mean, what's it going to be next?"

I nodded. "But so far no crime has been committed."

"Trespassing is a crime." Lia crossed her arms. "Tell me the truth. Do you know who's doing this? Do you have any idea?"

"Of course not."

"Why do I feel like the message is true? That you got some girl knocked up? And now she wants us both to know."

"It's not that," I said.

"Then why don't you want to report it?"

"Fine. I will."

After Lia went to her shoot, I phoned the local station. An hour later, a patrol car pulled up out front. Two uniforms stepped out of the car. Two guys, both of them looking about twenty.

I brought them around the side of the house, told them what happened.

Like I expected, they couldn't do much. They came into the house and looked at the doors and windows. One of them, the guy who did all the talking, suggested we buy a monitored alarm, and said he'd send someone to check the handle of the side gate for fingermarks. That way, they could see if there were any matches any on their database.

And that was it.

They left.

I knew Lia wasn't going to be thrilled. But what could I do? What could anyone do? I sat in the kitchen, staring out at the washing line swaying in the breeze.

That night we ate dinner silently. Lia had a fine appetite, but mine was completely gone.

"I'll stay up tonight," she said. "Since you're useless."

I ignored the barb. "Don't you have a shoot tomorrow?"

She looked at me for a long moment before replying. "I told you I don't."

"Oh, right. I forgot."

Lia shook her head. "I wonder what she sees in you."

"Who?"

"Your new girlfriend."

Through gritted teeth: "There's no new girlfriend, Lia."

"So who's pregnant?"

That was one question I couldn't answer.

After washing up, I went straight to bed. I was tired after losing so much sleep the previous days. I started reading another mystery novel, but keeping my eyes open was a struggle. I finally gave up on it after nodding off and dropping the book on my face.

I knew I'd be asleep at once. And I was.

I woke to find Lia shaking me.

Friday morning.

"Keith?"

"What?"

"You need to get up."

I rubbed my eyes and looked at Lia's face, half scared and half guilty.

"What's wrong?"

She said, "I… I fell asleep too."

"And?"

She didn't answer. Just beckoned for me to come.

I got out of bed and followed her downstairs. I knew what was coming. I just wasn't sure what new demented form it would take. Had our stalker got *I'M PREGNANT* printed on business cards? Was there a plane in the sky, writing the words in smoke? Had they planted flowers in the garden, spelling out the message?

"Something came," Lia said. "I haven't looked inside."

The front door was open and a cardboard box sat on the doorstep. It was about two feet by two feet by two feet. There was no address written on it.

There was a smattering of red droplets on the outside of the box. A whimper came from inside.

Lia and I exchanged a look.

"Where's Jack?" I said.

Lia put her hand to her mouth. I guessed that meant she hadn't seen him. My pulse sped up. I used my key to tear the sticky tape.

Jack lay on his side in the box, his white fur a mass of blood. He blinked but didn't get up. I didn't think he could.

"Call the vet," I said. "Tell them I'm on the way there."

SIX

I had to leave Jack with the vet. I was told he needed urgent surgery to try and patch up his wounds, and it would take time. There was no point hanging around. More to the point, I didn't want to hear the details of his stab wounds. I hated any kind of cruelty to animals. So I went home and told Lia. We stood in the hallway and hugged.

She'd brought the box into the hall. It was resting on a plastic bag, to stop Jack's blood staining the carpet.

"What's happening to us?" Lia said.

"I don't know."

"I don't want to spend the day at home. I'm going to meet my sister."

"Okay."

"Look in the box. I saw it after you took Jack out of it."

I'M PREGNANT was written in blood on the cardboard base. I'd been in such a hurry earlier, trying to get Jack to my car, that I hadn't noticed.

I felt like those two words were going to haunt me forever. It was like I was stuck inside some kind of ever-repeating nightmare.

Lia left to see her sister, and I headed to work.

I tried not to think about what had happened. I couldn't concentrate on the work, but my colleagues thought I was still ill, after my excuse the previous day, and they cut me some slack.

Lia kept texting me, but it was lunchtime before I got an update.

The operation was over. Jack was in recovery, but he'd been badly hurt and I should be prepared for the worst.

I got another call just as I left the office for the day.

Jack hadn't made it.

I was sitting at the kitchen table, crying like a baby when Lia arrived home. She was laden down with shopping bags from boutiques. But her composure broke as soon as she saw me.

I could hardly speak. Jack had been part of my life for years, before Lia and I were even married, and I felt more upset than I would have expected. It wasn't like Jack had ever shown me much affection.

Lia wrapped her arms around me. She smelled like perfume and lip gloss.

"Sorry, Keith. I know how much you loved him."

She started to kiss me, but I pulled away.

"How's your sister?"

Lia shrugged. “She’s her usual self. Nagged me again about taking up pilates, yoga, all that stuff. Said it would help my stress levels.”

“She only wants the best for you.”

“You know what would help my stress levels? Finding out who’s stalking us.”

“I’m working on it.”

After dinner, I drank a mug of strong coffee while Lia worked on her laptop at the kitchen table. I had a second cup around midnight and let Lia go to bed before me.

I sat in the darkness of the sitting room, the baseball bat in my hand. Every ten minutes, I walked to the back of the house and peered into the garden.

They weren’t going to get away this time.

I couldn’t stand the thought of another message arriving.

I planned to report everything the next morning. We’d heard nothing about the fingerprints, so I thought I’d better go to the station myself, to emphasise how concerned I was. I’d give the officers all the evidence I had. They might take my complaint more seriously after what had happened to Jack.

I started to gather everything together so I’d have it ready for the morning: the newspaper, the milk bottle, the T-shirt, the cardboard box Jack had come in. The only thing I couldn’t see was the first note, but I vaguely recalled Lia throwing it into the bin.

I made my way into the kitchen, being as quiet as I could. It was nearly four in the morning now. In the kitchen, we had a huge bin for general waste. The note must have been down at the bottom because I hadn't changed the bag since Monday. I took the bin liner out and set it down on the kitchen floor.

I gagged as I rooted through our waste for the past week. I couldn't see the sheet. I gave up being delicate and plunged my arm in. Stinking rubbish reached up almost to my armpit.

I felt around. My fingers closed around something hard. I couldn't think of what it might be, so I pulled it out. My hand and arm emerged from the rubbish absolutely filthy, but I ignored that. I'd grabbed a plastic tube. It took me a moment to realise what it was.

A pregnancy test.

Had the stalker broken in here and planted a pregnancy test in the bin? Or had Lia found it somewhere and thrown it away without telling me? I took it and walked out into the hall.

A figure was silently walking down the stairs, moving towards me through the darkness.

I just about had a heart attack, but managed to stifle the scream rising in my throat.

It was Lia.

Her eyes were open, staring ahead. She reached the bottom of the stairs and made for the front door.

"Lia? What are you doing?"

She continued on, not seeming to hear me. Was it possible that she still asleep? She opened the door and walked outside in her bare feet. She had her set of car keys in her hand.

I followed after her as if in a daze.

She walked to my car. Raising the key, she began to scratch letters into the paintwork of the driver's door.

I moved closer.

"Lia?"

Nothing. No response.

She kept scratching.

"Lia? Are you okay?"

When she had finished, she walked back inside the house and closed the door. I stood in the driveway, feeling stunned.

I'M PREGNANT, was scratched into my car door.

I went back into the house. Lia was nowhere to be seen, so I made my way up to our bedroom. She was in bed again, her eyes closed. The keys sat on the bedside unit next to her phone.

I was too freaked out to get into bed beside her so I went back downstairs and sat on the couch.

I wondered how long Lia's bizarre sleep activities had been going on. Had she been sleepwalking the whole six months we'd been married? Or had the pregnancy set it off? Did she consciously know she was pregnant?

What if she had taken the test while she was asleep?

The horrifying realisation struck me: she'd killed Jack while she was asleep. Not only that. She'd then sealed him in a box and left him on the doorstep.

It freaked me out at first, and then made my heard hurt, but I comforted myself with the thought that at least I'd got to the bottom of it. I'd lost Jack, but the mystery was solved. And tomorrow, Lia and I could talk to someone, find a sleep specialist to help her.

I was hot, almost feverish though it was the middle of the night. Maybe it was because of all the stress. I took my T-shirt off so I could cool down.

I lay on the couch, just thinking, until the sun came up and I started to feel safe.

Then my eyes became heavy and I fell asleep.

SEVEN

I had dreams, terrible dreams, and at some point they blurred into reality. I woke up to find Lia screaming in my face.

"Keith? Oh my god, Keith. Please be okay."

It felt like I was coming out of a thick fog.

I was confused. Then I thought, *I know what Lia will do. She'll lead me out to the car and point out the damage to the paintwork. And I'll explain my discovery from last night.*

This all passed through my mind in a flash.

Then I opened my eyes.

It was morning and I knew at once that something was very wrong.

Lia stood over me, dressed in loose jeans and a white blouse. She was covered in blood.

Had she been hurt? What was happening?

I tried to speak but no words came out. Just a wet gasp. I lifted my hands and saw that they were covered in blood.

There was a look of horror on Lia's face. She was in floods of tears. She tried to come closer. I shrank back.

"Keith, I've called an ambulance."

"You…"

"Save your strength, Keith. It's going to be okay." She shook her head. "We're going to find out who's doing this. I swear to god."

It took all the effort I could muster to get up off the couch. It was a bad idea. I was so light-headed I could barely stay on my feet.

"Keith, sit down! You have to let me put pressure on that neck wound."

I staggered towards the mirror over the fireplace and looked at my reflection. Aside from a savage puncture wound to my neck, bloody lines had been cut into my bare chest. They formed big, nasty letters. The words were backwards in the mirror, but I knew what they said.

The same two damn words.

"I'll find this monster," Lia said. "I promise."

I sank to the floor and Lia cradled me like a baby as everything went dark.

The Field

ONE

Jennifer O'Connell led her brothers onto the mud path which was their usual shortcut across the field. The ground was dry and cracked from the sun, and the air smelled of cut grass. Behind her, Martin, the older of her brothers, sneezed.

Jennifer turned and backhanded him across the face.

After a month, she was sick of his hayfever. This was the first year he'd had it and, as far as Jennifer was concerned, it better be his last.

Martin touched his cheek and gave Jennifer a dirty look, but said nothing.

Since turning eleven, he'd grown taller than her, stretching every day. Even his brown hair had become long. But at thirteen, Jennifer still had authority based on age.

Paul, the nine-year-old, traipsed silently behind them like a little duckling.

They were all dressed in their secondhand school uniforms. Grey trousers, grey jumpers, and white shirts. Jennifer's clothes didn't even fit. Only her handbag, made of pink canvas and brown leather, brought her any pleasure. And she'd had to shoplift that.

She straightened her back, checked that her dark ponytail was still tight, and continued across the field, ignoring the roar of a ride-on-mower. The machine, on the other side of the field, looked like a small tractor. Blue paint was flaking off its body and she could see dirt caked around the wheels.

The field was in the rough shape of a diamond, bordered on all sides by walls at the back of suburban gardens. There was nothing in the field but grass and a few sad-looking birch trees growing close to the wall. A concrete path meandered pointlessly along one side of the field. Hence the shortcut.

Jennifer could see her bedroom window from here but they couldn't get into the house from the back. They had to pass down a lane between two houses, then walk up Elm Drive to reach the front.

The mower turned and began to move towards the children. Jennifer caught sight of the driver. He was a big, meaty guy with earmuffs that sank into his hair. A cigarette stuck out of his beard.

"He's coming this way," Martin said, and snorted snot up his nose. "We should move."

Jennifer shielded her eyes from the sun. "Are you kidding me?"

Her brother was such a chicken. Just a big, lanky chicken.

Jennifer took out her packet of gum and folded a stick into her mouth. Sometimes gum helped take the edge off her hunger. There had been times when she thought she'd go mad from thinking about food. These days, if she got really hungry, she stole something to eat.

The mower got closer.

"We should step aside," Martin said.

Even over the engine noise, Jennifer could hear the fear in his voice. It made her want to hit him again.

Paul didn't say a word.

The mower had nearly reached them. Jennifer's eardrums felt like they were about to explode. She could hardly see a thing with the sun in her eyes.

"Get out of the way, you little bastards!" the man on the mower roared.

The cigarette flapped up and down when he spoke.

Jennifer ignored him.

She kept walking.

Inside her itchy polyester trousers, her legs were thin as sticks. The mower could crush her so easily. The driver wouldn't even feel a bump if he hit her.

Martin jogged towards the path while Paul's gaze shifted uncertainly between his brother and his sister.

Jennifer chewed her gum and kept walking.

The mower kept coming.

The engine roar grew louder. At the last second, the driver veered to the side.

"Stupid brats," he shouted.

Jennifer showed him her middle finger. He stared at it like he'd never seen one before. Then he brought his machine to a halt and jumped down to the ground. His belly wobbled as he stormed over to her.

"What was that?" he shouted.

Jennifer said nothing. She saw a woman emerge from the lane between the houses. She was pushing a buggy and juggling a coffee and a phone.

Mower Man said, "You kids get off the grass."

"Up yours," Jennifer said.

The guy's face turned a shade pinker. "The hell did you just say to me?"

He stepped closer, grabbed Jennifer by her shoulder, his fingers digging into her flesh.

Jennifer screamed as loud as she could. A high-pitched shriek that she reserved for moments like this. Mower Man let go of her at once and took a step back. He glanced at the lady across the field. She was staring at him hard.

Mower Man muttered something which sounded a lot like, *Fuck you all anyway*, then walked back to his machine and got on. He drove away without looking back.

Jennifer continued walking. Paul followed. Martin fell in behind them. He sneezed again and this time he shot his sister a wary look.

TWO

At the moment, home was a two-storey house, its walls covered in white plaster, its roof covered in blood-red tiles. It had a room for their mother, Val, one for Jennifer, and another for the boys. There was a patch of dead grass at the front and a thriving weed-garden at the back. It was the nicest place they'd lived all year.

Val was passed out on the leather couch in the sitting room. An episode of some soap opera played silently on the TV. A half-empty glass of white wine sat on the table next to the couch. A five-litre wine box sat on the carpet, making refills easy.

This was pretty much typical of how Val had been since Dad went to prison. Jennifer called him *Dad*, but Val was never *Mom*. Now Val was all they had. Pity. Jennifer always preferred her father.

"I'm hungry," Paul whispered.

Jennifer led him and Martin into the kitchen. This place had a big fridge-freezer. She found a pepperoni pizza in there – which was a minor miracle – and put it in the oven.

Bob, the guy who owned the place, had a fiancé but he liked to come by and see Val at the weekend. She didn't have much to do the rest of the week, though she said she was looking for a job. Jennifer wouldn't have trusted Val to clean a toilet, so she wasn't holding her breath that anyone else would either. In any case, Bob seemed happy enough letting them stay in the house for now.

The three O'Connell kids were silent while they waited for the oven to heat.

Jennifer decided they'd go back to the field later, and she'd stuff grass into Martin's mouth and nose. Then he'd think twice before making her look bad in front of anyone ever again.

THREE

Val woke up while the kids were eating dinner around the kitchen table. Jennifer heard her yawn and stretch in the sitting room. Maybe the pepperoni smell of the pizza had wafted to the next room. Jennifer started chewing faster. It would be just like Val to want a slice.

Jennifer had divided the pizza in six. She'd kept two slices for herself, given Paul two, and let Martin have one. She'd dropped Martin's second slice into the bin while he watched. Would he be hungry enough to eat it from the bin? That kind of question had always fascinated her.

And Martin did. He pulled the pizza slice out of the bin, gave it a quick wipe with the back of his hand, and then devoured it greedily.

"I'm still starving," Martin said after swallowing it.

"You can have some of mine," Paul said. He always ate slowly.

Jennifer shook her head. “No, he can’t. Martin made his choice in the field. He chose to run away.”

Martin scowled.

Once she was an adult, Jennifer would earn a lot of money, and be able to eat as many pizzas as she wanted, and she’d never share with anyone again.

“I hate you,” Martin said, just as Val appeared in the doorway. Her dressing gown hung open, showing a peach-coloured camisole underneath.

“Hey,” Val said. “When did you all get home?”

“Could you put your tits away?” Jennifer said.

Val glared at her. “Don’t be a smartass.”

“I suppose Bob is coming tonight?” Jennifer said.

It was a Friday, and that was his usual evening. His fiancé was a waitress and she always worked a late shift on Fridays.

“Oh, shit. That’s right. I need to have a shower. You guys make yourself scarce when Bob gets here. The last time, he said you guys were too noisy.”

Jennifer remembered. They’d been making a racket because they couldn’t stand the dying-pig sound of Val and Bob having sex.

“Don’t worry.” Jennifer said. “We’ll go out.”

FOUR

When the kids heard Bob's Audi pull up in the driveway, they were watching TV with Val. She got to her feet at once.

"Time to go out and play."

Jennifer was happy to oblige. Bob was a creep, even if he did own a nice car and two houses. He hadn't even earned any of that stuff, just inherited it. Pretty much the only time he talked to her or her brothers was to boast about his golfing skills, though he'd only taken up the sport since he came into money.

Val thought he was going to keep letting them live there rent-free, but Jennifer knew better. It was only a matter of time until he got bored of Val and kicked them out.

Jennifer led Paul and Martin outside, ignoring Bob's "Want to see my new clubs?" as he stepped out of the car.

They walked to the field. The sky was still bright and the air smelled like barbecued chicken.

When they emerged from the lane leading to the field, Jennifer stopped. She stood at the edge of the grass and stared across the field. A faded one-man tent had been put up in the corner. As they watched, a skinny man in a grey tracksuit got out of it. Maybe he was in his forties or fifties. He was bald and he had one of those faces with deep lines.

He began setting up a gas stove outside his tent.

"Who's that?" Paul said. "Why is he camping there?"

Jennifer stared at the man with the lined face.

"He's not camping, moron. He's homeless."

Jennifer set off across the grass. The barbecue smell seemed to be coming from every direction. All the neighbours must have been cooking. Jennifer's mouth began to water.

"I don't want to go near him," Martin said. "He looks weird."

Jennifer turned and stared at him until he lowered his eyes. She walked on and Martin didn't speak again.

Baldy ducked into his tent, then came out again. Up close, Jennifer saw that his skin was blotchy pink and he had eyes the colour of rain.

"Clear off," Baldy said.

His voice was gruff.

"Who are you?" Jennifer asked. "Where did you come from?"

"Never mind that. Piss off."

"We usually play here," Paul said in a small voice. Since Val moved them here, they'd spent hours every day sitting in this corner of the field. They never tried to fit in with the other kids anywhere they lived, as they knew they'd be moving again soon.

Baldy took a step forward. His knees and elbows were bent, so he came at them in an apish manner. Paul shrank back, gripping the back of Jennifer's T-shirt.

Baldy said, "I'm here now. Play somewhere else."

He darted forward suddenly. Just a few inches, but enough to scare Martin and Paul, who grabbed Jennifer's T-shirt even tighter and gasped. Baldy's eyes lit up in amusement.

The opening of the tent was unzipped. Jennifer saw a pile of filthy clothes inside and a bottle of some kind of spirit.

Jennifer stepped forward, folding her arms, and trying her best to look authoritative. "We're not going anywhere."

"Is that right?"

Baldy darted forward and grabbed Jennifer's bag. He tore it off her shoulder, snapping the strap.

"Nice," he sneered, revealing two rows of pointy, yellow teeth. "Any money in it?"

Jennifer's chest swelled with rage. She'd taken the risk of shoplifting to get this bag. She didn't want to lose it.

"Give that back."

Baldy ignored her and unzipped the bag. He started rooting through the contents, then emptied the whole thing out onto the grass. Lip balm, make-up, a hand mirror, a small purse with 36 cents in it. He scowled.

"A lot of bollocks."

He kicked her stuff away from him, then lobbed the bag into his tent.

"Hey. Give that back," Jennifer said.

The man smiled. "Go get it."

Jennifer knew she was being challenged. She didn't want to go inside the tent, but she couldn't back down. So she took a step forward. Paul tugged on her arm. Trying to hold her back. She shook him off and took another step.

Up close, Baldy stank of sweat and something worse. Jennifer felt his hot breath on her cheek. She passed by him, got on her hands and knees and entered the tent.

Her handbag had landed on top of a mound of Baldy's clothes. She reached for it, leaning across Baldy's bedding, which she really didn't want to touch. She had to stretch, her right arm out as far as it could go.

Her fingers had just grazed the bag's surface when Baldy grabbed her from behind.

Jennifer struggled and tried to shout out but he clamped his hand over her mouth.

"Do you like it?" he hissed into her ear. "Do you like it, little girl?"

Jennifer heard Martin and Paul outside. Their voices were coming closer.

"Hey, let her go!"

"Jennifer!"

Baldy's grip tightened.

For the first time, terror gripped her.

He's going to murder me, she thought. *And Martin and Paul won't stop him.*

The idea appalled her. It also gave her a burst of energy. She drove her elbow behind her as hard as she could. The blow connected with Baldy's throat and he released her at once.

She scrambled out of the tent. Paul and Martin were right outside. They hurried away together. Jennifer didn't look back until they'd crossed the grass and reached the path. She was breathing hard and she needed to stop for a moment.

She looked back.

Baldy was standing outside his tent. A triumphant smile played across his lips. He held Jennifer's bag above his head.

He shouted, "I'll keep this. You can come get it any time you like."

Jennifer hurried away, leaving her brothers running behind her. She didn't want them to see her cry.

"Are you okay?" Paul said.

She kept walking, wiping the tears away.

"Yeah."

"Where can we play now?" Paul asked.

"It's no big deal," Martin said. "We can find somewhere else."

Jennifer shook her head. "No way. That's our field. And I want my bag."

"So what are we going to do?"

Jennifer had an idea.

FIVE

At 2 am, the kids snuck out of their bedroom. They'd walked around the streets until about ten, then come home and hung around in Jennifer's room. Jennifer was certain that Val and Bob wouldn't be shifting now. She could hear Val snoring.

She hoped that by now Baldy would be settled for the night too.

Jennifer found the keys to Bob's car in his jacket, which was hung over the bannister at the bottom of the stairs. The house had an alarm but Val never set it. The kids opened the door silently, and stepped out into the night.

Jennifer unlocked the car and popped the boot. She selected a driver from the set of golf clubs there. Paul and Martin gazed at her with fearful eyes.

"For protection," she explained.

She took Bob's leather golf gloves too and put them on. Bob was such a dummy, he thought you had to wear two of them when you played. Jennifer didn't even like golf, but she'd seen the pros, and they only wore a glove on one hand.

She closed the boot and they began walking towards the field.

"I'm scared," Paul said.

She handed him and Martin rain ponchos and put one on herself.

"So he won't recognise us."

They started off across the grass.

The moon shone onto the field. There was no one around. A light breeze provided the only movement.

The driver felt heavy in Jennifer's hand.

She swung it while they walked, getting a feel for it.

She put a finger to her lips as they crept closer to the tent. No light came from inside. She took a breath and started to unzip the opening. The sound seemed incredibly loud. Her heart was beating madly. She didn't stop, though. Finally the flap was fully open.

It was dark inside, but Jennifer saw Baldy lying on his side, his head resting on his arm. His head was at the other end of the tent, his feet at the near end.

She poked him lightly with the golf club.

No reaction.

"Pull him out," Jennifer whispered to her brothers.

Martin whispered, "What?"

She hadn't mentioned anything about that.

"We need to scare him. Grab his legs and pull him out on my count."

Looking uncertain, Paul and Martin ducked into the tent. They each took hold of a leg.

Jennifer hissed, "Three, two, one. *Pull.*"

The boys grabbed Baldy's legs and pulled him through the flap. But they collided in the narrow space. Martin knocked Paul down, then fell over his own feet.

Baldy woke with a gasp, half in and half out of the tent.

"Pull him out," Jennifer hissed.

Baldy scrambled to get to his feet, but Martin grabbed one leg. Paul grabbed the other and they pulled. Baldy came clear of the tent.

Jennifer stepped forward. She drew back the club, gripping it firmly with both hands, and swung the driver with all her might, smashing it into the side of Baldy's skull.

He stopped struggling. Stopped doing anything.

It was comical, really.

"Oh god," Martin gasped.

"Is he alright?" Paul said.

Jennifer stepped closer and examined him. The driver had left an indent in the side of Baldy's head. That spot was a mass of gore, and she thought she could see fragments of skull poking out of the wound. She touched it, getting blood on the gloves.

"Of course he's not alright. He's dead, you moron. I just can't believe it was so easy."

She ducked into the tent and found her handbag. Then she searched around for Beardy's wallet. He didn't seem to have one, but she found a small roll of bank notes tied together with a rubber band. In the middle of the cash, there was a photo of a woman. Jennifer found a phone nearby too. She took them all with her and ducked out of the tent.

They hurried home.

Jennifer's heart was racing.

When they got back to their driveway, Jennifer left the bloody golf club on the backseat of Bob's Audi. She threw one of the golf gloves in there too.

All was quiet in the house. Jennifer took the rain ponchos from the two boys.

"Go to bed," she whispered.

They obeyed, creeping silently upstairs to their room.

Jennifer put Baldy's phone on silent mode, then slipped it into the pocket of Bob's jacket, which hung over the bannister. She also put the roll of notes and the photograph of the lady in there too, together with the second glove.

Then she went into the kitchen and closed the door, so Val and Bob wouldn't hear her wash Baldy's blood off the ponchos.

SIX

The next day was Saturday. Martin and Paul got up around eleven and sat in front of the TV to watch cartoons. Val's door was shut and Bob's Audi was still in the driveway.

Jennifer tried to fix them all some cereal but the milk came out of the carton in a solid, sour-smelling mass. So the three of them sat on the floor in front of the TV, eating bowls of dry cereal. It was a crappy breakfast. The clusters of cereal just tasted like sugar and gave Jennifer a headache.

I'm going to be rich when I grow up, she thought. *And I'm never going to eat cereal again.*

She promised herself she'd never live like Val, once she was old enough to live by herself. She figured she'd ditch Martin. She hadn't decided yet if she wanted to keep Paul around. Probably not. She didn't want anyone reminding her of this time in her life.

Jennifer waited until noon before she went outside with her brothers. After everyone was clear on their story, they went to the field.

An ambulance, a white van, and two patrol cars were parked on the grass around Baldy's tent. The forensics people wore white overalls and face masks. They'd covered Baldy's horrible little tent with their own one, a large white structure that blocked the scene from view. Dozens of people were standing on the path, watching. A couple of uniformed officers prevented them getting any closer.

Jennifer walked over to the closest officer, who was a tall lady with bright blonde hair tied back in a ponytail. A pair of handcuffs hung from her belt.

She smiled at Jennifer. "Hello, sweetheart. You step back now."

Jennifer put on her most innocent voice. "What happened?"

"Nothing you need to worry about. You and your little friends run along now."

"Can we play here?"

"Not today."

Jennifer hesitated, then said, "Will Bob be in trouble?"

"What do you mean, sweetheart? Who's Bob?"

Paul said, "He's our mom's boyfriend."

"Well, why would he be in trouble?"

"He doesn't like homeless people." Jennifer lowered her voice. "He said he'd make the man in the tent go away."

The officer's smile dimmed a little.

"He said that?"

"Yeah."

"Was he here last night?"

Jennifer shrugged. "I don't know but he left the house in the middle of the night. We live just around the corner."

The officer nodded evenly. She wasn't smiling at all now.

"Where exactly do you live, sweetheart?"

"I can show you."

Jennifer, Paul and Martin got a ride home in a patrol car, which was fun. The officer they'd spoken to was named Gina. Her partner was a big man she called Tom, who didn't speak a word. Gina asked a few more questions in the car and Jennifer did all the answering.

As they walked up the driveway, Jennifer pointed to the Audi.

"That's Bob's car."

Gina looked inside. She frowned and turned to her partner. He looked through the window too, then walked down the driveway and spoke into his radio.

Gina said, "Do you have a key to your door, sweetheart?"

"Sure."

Jennifer opened the door and went inside. Through the doorway to the sitting room, she could see Val and Bob lying on the couch together. Normally Jennifer hated it when they did that, but now she was pleased. Bob was smoking a joint.

"Come on in," Jennifer said.

She stepped into the hallway, with Gina following right behind her.

"Holy shit," Bob said, jumping up as soon as he clocked the uniform. "Who are you?"

“I’ve got some questions for you too,” Gina said.

Bob stubbed out the joint in the ashtray while Gina turned to Jennifer. She flashed her a bright smile.

“Why don’t you let me talk to the grown-ups alone.”

Jennifer shrugged. Paul and Martin followed her upstairs.

The three of them sat down on the floor.

“I’m scared,” Martin said.

“Don’t be stupid,” Jennifer told him. “Bob’s the one who should be scared. I wonder if he’ll meet Dad in prison. Wouldn’t that be fun?”

“I guess.”

Jennifer got a needle and thread, and tried to sew the leather strap back onto her handbag, which she’d cleaned the previous night. It didn’t work and she figured she’d need to use a sewing machine. That was okay. She threw the bag in her bin. They had their field, which was what mattered. And no one was going to take it away from them.

Dead Funny

ONE

On Wednesday evening, Jessica Roberts stood outside Burke's Pub for fifteen minutes before she found the courage to step inside. She would have stayed on the street longer, reading an article about the murders on her phone, but her hands were numb from the chilly February air, and she didn't even have a drink.

She stepped inside the pub, the cloying smell of beer hitting her at once, the buzz of conversation so loud that it stopped her for a second, making her wonder if she really wanted to do this.

Burke's was full of young professionals who worked near Grafton Street. The pub was long and narrow. A mahogany bar ran its length. The wall opposite the bar was lined with stools. No room for tables, so a wooden shelf ran along the wall.

As Jessica entered, the TV on the wall sprang to life. The pub filled with the booming voice of a football commentator.

She felt a nervous chill, thinking of the killings, one in Paris and one in Milan. Both had taken place over the previous month, and people were starting to talk about a connection. A roving killer, who liked to slit throats.

Jessica took a breath. She needed to get into the right frame of mind before she headed downstairs to the comedy club. According to her watch, she was due onstage in seven minutes. She didn't want to go there straight away. A gin and tonic would steady her nerves, and they needed steadying.

My first ever gig.

She hadn't told her family or friends about it, in case she bombed, and that was a distinct possibility. She'd had a tedious day of data entry at the bank, and she wasn't feeling funny.

She squeezed through a group of men, holding pints of beer in front of their bellies, standing motionless like penguins before the TV screen. She pushed up her glasses as they started to slide down her nose. They'd become loose and were driving her crazy.

Her spirits sank when she saw the queue at the bar. A young man was ordering and an older man stood behind him. Jessica checked her watch. Five minutes left.

"Hey," she called, waving to the barman.

He glanced at her, then pointed to the queue.

"Come on. I work here," Jessica said. "I'm in a hurry."

He didn't take the bait. Not surprising, as it wasn't strictly true. Burke's wasn't paying her. She was getting something more valuable than money for her routine: exposure. She couldn't figure out why her landlord didn't accept it as payment for rent.

"What would you like?" The handsome young man standing at the top of the queue turned around and smiled at her. His accent sounded like Washington, but he didn't look like a tourist. His blue shirt was too sharp. His lustrous brown hair was slicked back, not a hair out of place. She guessed he was in town for a conference or a business meeting.

"G and T," she said.

He turned to the barman, adding her drink to his order.

The man who stood between them rolled his eyes, but Jessica ignored him.

"Thanks," she shouted.

"What's your name?" her new friend asked, revealing two rows of gleaming white teeth.

"Jessica. You?"

"I'm Mark."

He stuck out his hand. When she shook it, his skin was dry and warm. The man standing between them shook his head. More people were joining the queue, so she backed away to the wall behind. She took a stool, leaning a possessive elbow on the shelf.

After a minute, Mark brought her drink over. He'd got a Coke for himself.

"Just a second," he said.

He set down the drinks and went back to the bar to grab three more. He brought them over to his friends at the end of the bar. Jessica watched the way he walked back to her, moving around other customers with an ease she envied. He was like a cat.

When he returned to her, she held out a note for the drink.

"Or would you prefer PayPal?"

Mark smiled.

"It's on me," he shouted over the buzz of conversation.

"Thanks."

"Are you alone?"

Jessica nodded, sank half her drink in one gulp.

Mark said, "Well, you're not now. Come join me and my friends."

"I can't," she said. She nodded to the sign on the wall above us. JOIN US FOR OUR COMEDY CLUB EVERY WEDNESDAY EVENING. FREE ENTRY. "That's me."

He read the poster with what looked like genuine interest.

"Cool," he said, sitting down on the stool next to her. "I might check it out."

Jessica nodded and finished her drink. "Do."

"It seems you need a little Dutch courage?"

"Something like that. Thanks for the gin."

Getting to her feet, she gave him a nod, then walked to the side of the pub and down the steps to the club.

Her nerves were worse than they had before the gin and tonic.

TWO

The staircase leading to the comedy club was at the side of the small stage. The basement was dim and Jessica could hear the buzz of the sound system.

Thomas Martin was on the stage. With his beard and bare ankles, he looked like a typical hipster. Jessica was sure his jokes were artisan, organic and locally sourced. Probably free range too. But his sense of humour was hard to appreciate. He glanced Jessica's way as she appeared, momentarily distracting him.

The stage was raised about a foot above the floor, so it didn't offer much protection from the audience if they decided to attack. The basement room had a smaller floor plan than the bar upstairs. Still, the owners managed to fit about fifteen small tables in, and a few stools around each one. On every table, a candle glowed in a blood-red glass.

Only a handful of tables were occupied.

There was no backstage – at least, none that Burke's wanted to share with comedy hopefuls, so Jessica perched on a stool at the nearest table.

Onstage, Thomas was finishing up his usual act. Jessica had heard him twice before and it was always the same: the kind of jokes you find in Christmas crackers. Baffling, but maybe he was trying to carve a niche for himself with the retirement-home crowd.

"Did I tell you that my parents raise owls? It's true. But there's no point asking for one. They don't give a hoot."

Dead silence.

Jessica cringed, but inwardly she was pleased. Her act would seem funnier by comparison.

Thomas smiled. He said, "How about one more joke before I go?"

"You suck!" someone shouted.

Jessica looked around but couldn't tell who'd said it. Her pulse began to race. She'd hoped for a reactive audience, but not like that.

She wondered how Thomas would handle it. She could make out a sheen of sweat on his forehead.

His eyes darted around as if he'd lost his train of though. "Um alright… maybe that's enough. I think we're out of time. You've been a wonderful audience. Thank you very much," he said. "Have a great evening. Thank you."

He walked off the stage in dead silence, stopping to pick up a pint left at the corner of the stage. Jessica got to her feet and came up behind him.

"Tough crowd," she said.

Thomas swallowed half his pint. "Worst I've ever had. Are you the girl who's up next?"

She nodded. "Jessica. I'm not sure I want to go on now."

"You might have better luck with them than I did. Which wouldn't be hard. Just don't let them smell fear."

"Are you sticking around?"

Thomas shook his head.

"I don't want to spend another second in this shithole," he said, wiping the sweat from his face with his shirtsleeve. "But good luck."

It would have been nice to have someone announce her, but Burke's didn't provide an MC, and Thomas was already hurrying up the stairs with his almost-empty glass.

She took a breath.

Just don't let them smell fear.

She could do that.

THREE

Jessica stepped onto the stage, and turned, squinting in the glare of the spotlight. The powerful light made her feel like sneezing. It also made her feel hot.

She gazed out at the audience. A few bored glances. Mostly, people kept talking and drinking. Their voices were low. The space had an eerie atmosphere.

She checked out the kind of people who were sitting at the various tables: three career women with cocktails, an older husband and wife sitting stony-faced, two young men drinking stout, a woman by herself, perhaps waiting for a friend, and a guy by himself, possibly with no friends.

Not ideal. Jessica would have liked to see more young couples, and groups of friends who were still sober enough to appreciate wit.

Perhaps a confrontational approach would work best with this audience.

She walked up to the microphone and took a pack of antibacterial wipes from her pocket. Removing one, she began to clean the microphone and the stand.

"Not that I'm fussy," she said into mic. "Good evening, folks. I'm Jessica. I'm not going to ask how you're doing tonight because I don't care."

Absolute silence.

A movement in the darkness at her side startled her. It was Richard, another comedian, coming down the stairs from the bar. He was due on after Jessica. Richard gave her a thumbs-up and sat down.

"Okay," Jessica said into the mic. She looked around the room. "It's good to be here. This is a beautiful funeral home."

"You suck," a man shouted. One of the two men drinking stout. They cracked up laughing.

"Thanks for coming," she said.

"You still suck."

She wiped her clammy hands on her shirt.

More people were coming downstairs from the bar.

How could anyone concentrate with all these distractions? Who chose to put a stage right beside a damn staircase?

One of the newcomers was her American friend, Mark. With him was an anorexic young woman and an older lady with a scornful eye. Both of them were neat in a smart-casual kind of way. At the back of the pack was a huge mountain of a man in a black shirt and jeans. With his bald head and bulging muscles, he looked like a professional wrestler.

"Join the party," Jessica said. "We're having a great time here."

Mark smiled and led his group to a table near the front.

"Okay," Jessica said. "Let's introduce ourselves. Me? I'm here to torture you for the next fifteen minutes." She pointed at the heckler. "This is Obnoxious Drunk Number One. His mother didn't give him enough love, and now he hates women."

The guy's friend broke out laughing, but no one else cracked a smile. Obnoxious Drunk Number One said, "Haha," in an unfunny voice, then added "Four-eyed bitch."

A wave of irritation shot up Jessica's spine. Her glasses had begun to slide down her nose. She pushed them up again.

Take it easy. He's just an idiot. Return to the regular jokes. Stop picking a fight with the audience.

"So, I was honoured when Burke's invited me to perform here tonight. This is my first show and..."

The two drunk men were talking to each other in loud voices, completely ignoring her. They were so loud that she forgot the joke she had been about to make.

"Hey," Jessica said, "You two. What are you talking about that's so important?"

Obnoxious Drunk Number One said. "Piss off."

"Any other comments?"

"You suck," his friend shouted.

"Is that all you can say? You can learn to expand your vocabulary. Many libraries have adult literacy programs. It's nothing to be ashamed of."

A murmur of laughter. Jessica scanned the rest of the audience. "Okay, let's see who else we've got here. There's Mr and Mrs Miserable," she said, looking at the older, stony-faced couple. "They ran out of things to say to each other in 1975. They're probably here to steal my material and use it in conversation."

A louder murmur of laughter, and embarrassed looks from the old couple. Jessica hadn't planned to pick on people. She didn't like mean-spirited comedians, but this audience had forced Thomas Martin off the stage, and she wasn't going to let that happen to her. She turned to Mark's table.

"Here's my American friend, who bought me a drink upstairs. He's so squeaky clean, he's probably a serial killer. I'm guessing his hobbies include making purses from baby goats. Maybe eating pineal glands."

Mark smiled, and the rest of the audience laughed a little, except Mark's friends.

Jessica pointed at the big bald man and said, "I don't believe those muscles are real. This guy is on steroids or else those are inflatable. I guess your sugar mommy here likes a good six-pack," Jessica added, giving the older lady a conspiratorial wink.

The woman's face paled. The younger woman with her looked unhappy too.

But that wasn't what worried Jessica.

The big man was.

He jumped to his feet, his face twisted into a terrifying expression. He looked like he wanted to tear Jessica limb from limb.

Mark pulled his friend down, but the man was clearly still angry, and Jessica heard him say something chilling.

Going to make her pay.

FOUR

If anything worried Jessica more than germs and the threat of public humiliation, it was physical violence. She was sure the huge man, with the physique of a bodybuilder, had told Mark he was going to make Jessica pay.

And that didn't mean he planned to send her an invoice.

He was *angry*.

Jessica's stomach lurched at the thought of him rushing at her, those huge muscles of his flexing in preparation of tearing her head from her shoulders.

She dropped the mic and jumped down off the stage to the shriek of feedback over the speakers.

She ran up the steps to the pub as quickly as she could.

Ignoring everything around her, she hurried straight to the toilet. The place was empty. She ducked into the nearest stall and closed her eyes. She had always been very sensitive, especially to the sensation of fear, and now her stomach heaved.

Trying to hold back the urge to get sick, she forced herself to take a breath.

Be calm.

Take it easy.

But it was no good. The contents of her stomach came up in a rush. She bent over the bowl and vomited.

When it was all up, she wiped her mouth.

"Shit," she gasped.

She hadn't puked in a pub since she was eighteen. It hadn't become any more enjoyable in the decade since.

She took her phone out of the pocket of her jeans, thinking she'd check the next bus. She wanted to get out of there, to go home and hide away from the humiliation and the threat of violence.

Her hands were slick with sweat, and the phone slipped out of her grasp and fell into the toilet, landing in the dirty water with a splash.

Jessica leaned over and watched as it sank to the filthy ceramic at the bottom. *No.* That phone had *everything* on it. Her photos, her contacts, her ideas for jokes. All kinds of stuff.

Most people would probably have reached into the water and plucked it out, but Jessica couldn't bring herself to do that. The thought of all that filth, from so many people, over so many years – it was enough to make her queasy all over again.

Even if she had been able to force herself to reach in and grab it, there was no chance she'd ever be able to think of the phone as clean again. She'd never be able to set it down on the couch next to her, or put it on her bedside locker.

No way.

Never.

It was gone.

She took a moment to accept that.

At least things can't get any worse, Jessica thought.

That was when her glasses slid down her nose and fell into the bowl too.

FIVE

Like her phone, Jessica's glasses were everything to her. But even more so. Without them, the world was a blur of colours and shapes. She *needed* her glasses. But there was no way she was going to reach into a dirty pub toilet, fish them out, and put them back on her head.

No thanks.

Not that she was fussy, but she didn't feel like a bout of cholera.

Painful as the thought was, her phone and glasses were gone, as far as Jessica was concerned.

It wasn't the end of the world. She had spare glasses at home, though she'd have to buy a new phone. Or maybe not – she had five or six old ones in a drawer in her bedroom, all of them with various minor dysfunctions. Maybe she'd just get a new SIM card and try it in one of them.

She washed her hands at the sink, and rinsed the vomit taste out of her mouth, before leaving of the bathroom.

Football was still blaring from the TV screen on the wall. Men stood around, chatting and holding their pints. Everything was a blur. It was hard to even tell how far away things were.

Jessica pushed through the crowd, heading for the door, until a hand reached out of the mass of people and grabbed her wrist.

She jumped.

"Jessica? Are you okay?"

"Richard?" She squinted as the man drew closer. "Is that you?"

"Yeah." He laughed. "Where are your glasses?"

Richard was meant to go onstage after her. She wondered what he was doing upstairs.

"I lost them. I can't see a thing."

Richard whistled. "It's really not your night."

"Tell me about it. Why aren't you doing your act?"

"You know the bald guy in the audience? The one who got offended?"

Jessica swallowed. "What about him?"

"After you left, he went crazy and overturned a table. Broken glass everywhere. His friend calmed him down, but most of the audience had already left."

Her breathing turned shallow. She'd known that guy looked like trouble. Why did she have to bait him?

Jessica said, "Where is he now?"

“I’m not sure. Everyone left. There was no one for me to tell jokes to.” Richard shrugged. “I thought I’d watch the match for a while.”

“I have to go,” Jessica said.

“Okay. That’s probably best. You don’t want to run into that guy. I wonder where he went.”

Jessica did too.

SIX

Jessica hurried out of the pub. She pushed the door open so hard, it banged into a woman standing outside. She was sheltering from the rain that was now falling heavily. People hurried along the street with umbrellas up.

The woman swore. She looked at Jessica. "Oh, it's you. Don't give up the day job, love."

The woman laughed. Though she was a blur, her bright red top was familiar. One of the career women from the comedy club.

I hate these people, Jessica thought.

The streetlight was a blur of orange, the cars were white and red blurs. The people were dark blurs.

Jessica stepped into the rain. Her jacket that was too light. She'd worn it because she thought the green cotton jacket looked smart with her jeans, and she had wanted to look smart onstage. In the real world, it was useless. It didn't keep her warm and, after a few paces, the material was soaked.

She decided to go to the bus stop on nearby Dame Street. If she could find her way there, she'd be able to get a bus home to Tallaght.

She set off walking fast. She tripped a few times, but made it to the bus stop. Then she realised that, without her glasses, she couldn't read the digital display at the bus stop. And with her phone gone, she couldn't check that either.

She stood alone at the bus stop and waited.

A bus came and she realised she couldn't make out the number on the front. She held out her arm and made it stop.

The door opened with a *whoosh*.

Jessica stepped inside. "Excuse me?"

The driver was looking the other way, as if avoiding any customer interaction. He slowly turned and looked at her.

Jessica said, "What bus is this?"

"Can't you read?"

"No, I lost my glasses."

"Sixteen," he said.

"Sorry. Wrong one."

He sighed.

She got off, feeling bad that she'd wasted his time, but irritated at his attitude. The rain continued to pour down.

After a few minutes, an old lady came and stood next to Jessica. They got talking. The lady was waiting for the same bus, so Jessica relaxed a little, knowing she wouldn't miss her ride home. The woman even let Jessica stand under her umbrella. Jessica was taller so she held it over both of them.

Their bus came in less than a minute. Jessica got on and took a seat near the back. She stared out the window at the blurry cityscape.

The bus started to move off, when a man came running up and banged on the door. Jessica squinted at him. He was big and bald, and there was aggression in the way he moved.

It's him, Jessica thought. *The guy from the club.*

The man who had vowed to make her pay.

He'd followed her.

The man banged on the glass door so hard, Jessica thought he'd break it. But it held, and the driver ignored him. The bus moved away from the kerb.

The cars ahead were barely moving, so it was easy for the man to keep pace with the bus, running alongside it and continuing to smash his first against the door.

Everyone was watching now. Jessica sensed the nervous anticipation in the air.

Her nerves were fried. She squeezed her travel card tight in her hands and prayed.

Don't open the door. Please don't open the door.

SEVEN

Rain pounded against the window next to Jessica. The water ran down the glass in angry rivulets. Ahead, the traffic lights changed. Traffic began to move. The bus driver hit the accelerator and left the bald man behind.

Through the wall of the bus, over the sound of the engine, and the thrashing rain, Jessica heard the man howl in anger.

She realised she had been holding her breath, and let it out.

I'm okay.

I'm safe.

What a night.

She didn't have her glasses or her phone, she had indeed bombed at the comedy club, and the gin and tonic she'd drunk earlier felt oily and repulsive in her stomach – but so what? She had gotten away and was heading home.

A long bubble bath would fix her up. Maybe followed by a Netflix binge.

It was hard not to feel a little jumpy though. Every time someone came downstairs from the top deck, Jessica squinted at them warily.

For the majority of the journey, she gazed out the window, trying to identify any landmarks that would tell her where she was. Most buses have digital announcements now, telling passengers the location every minute or two, but this one didn't.

After forty-five minutes, Jessica thought the bus must be approaching her road. She stood up and pressed the bell. The driver pulled in, way past the stop.

Jessica stepped out onto the footpath.

The rain was still falling.

She watched the bus pull away and set off walking. She lived down the road, near a small line of shops.

She had only gone a few paces when another bus pulled in at the stop where she'd just got off.

The door opened.

A man got out.

A dark blur, with a bald head. He turned towards Jessica.

She couldn't see him clearly, but somehow she knew it was him.

The guy from the club.

She turned and ran. Only once did she look back, and she saw that the man was running too, coming right after her, his powerful legs working like a machine. He was gaining on her. With a rising sense of terror, she urged herself to run faster.

The ground was a blur beneath her. She hoped she wouldn't fall.

Jessica's house was on her left. She could have run in and shut the door, but then the guy would learn where she lived, and she didn't want that.

Instead she ran towards the shops.

The automatic door of the corner shop opened as she approached. The guy at the counter was a young Indian. She knew him to see, though she had never learned his name.

"Sorry," Jessica said, not even slowing. She knew where the back exit was. Employees were always out there, smoking. She ran around the side of the counter, and pushed the door. The metal screeched as it opened. Jessica found herself in an empty car park at the back of the shops.

Footsteps pounded behind her.

The man was catching up.

"Wait," he shouted.

Instead, she ran to her right, hoping to make her way around to the front again and lose him. As she reached the corner, a car screeched to a stop in front of her. Two headlights blazed, blinding her.

The back-left passenger door opened, and a familiar face appeared: Mark, the American who'd bought her a drink.

"Quick, get in."

She glanced behind. The bald man was coming up fast behind her. She'd never outrun him. This was her only hope. She scrambled around the side of the taxi and jumped in.

Mark leaned forward and spoke to the driver.

"Fifty euros if you get away from here fast."

Without a word, the driver accelerated hard, driving the car out onto the street and down the road.

They shot past Jessica's house and continued up the road. They'd gone a mile before Jessica caught her breath. Then she turned to Mark.

She said, "Your friend scared the hell out of me."

"I know, I'm sorry. There was no need for that."

"What's going on?"

Mark looked out the window. Leaning forward in his seat, he pointed to a quiet side road. He said to the driver, "Can you pull in there?"

The car turned down the road and came to a gentle stop.

Jessica's fear had given way to anger. "Mark, I'm talking to you. Why was your friend so offended?"

"He wasn't."

Suddenly there was a knife in Mark's hand. He reached around the driver and drew the knife across the man's throat. He had no chance to say anything before his blood started to spurt onto the windscreen.

Jessica wanted to scream but she was frozen in shock, not quite able to believe what she was seeing. The driver put his hands to his throat, but Jessica sensed that it was too late. There was so much blood.

"You were right about me," Mark said. He turned to Jessica and he had a big smile on his nice, wholesome face. His eyes were wide with excitement. "I know, comedians say a lot of things. They kid around. But sometimes they hit the nail on the head. And you did."

"What are you talking about?"

Mark turned in his seat, his grin widening as he did so.

"My friend wasn't offended by you. He was *worried* about you, because you were right about me.

And he knows what I'm like. They all do – my friends who were in the club tonight. They know what tickles my fancy. He wanted to warn you."

"Warn me?"

"We've had a lot of fun during our tour of Europe," Mark said. "My friends think I've been having too much fun. Drawing attention to us."

Jessica shook her head. No. It couldn't be.

She said, "I don't understand."

"I think you do."

She thought of the murders. The ones in Paris and Milan. The stabbing victims. Her stomach felt weak.

Mark smiled. "We all like to have a laugh, in our own way."

"No," Jessica said. "Your friend, he was angry. He said, 'Going to make her pay'."

"No, my friend said, "Don't make her pay'. But I'd already decided to punish you."

"Because I said you look like a serial killer?"

"No. Because when I bought you a drink and sat down next to you, you walked out on me. You left me alone and I looked like a loser."

Jessica's voice was a croak. "I'm sure no one was looking."

"My friends were. Anyway, that was when I thought about it first. And then when you called me a serial killer? That's when I decided for sure. Maybe it's not wise but…" Mark shrugged. "Sometimes I just can't resist."

The knife was a blur, but Jessica saw the blade gleam as it rushed at her.

Escalate

ONE

I was driving over a desolate patch of the Wicklow Mountains when it happened. The roads up there are twisty and narrow, and there's no public lighting. Dusk had just fallen. I'd flicked on my Ford Escort's headlights a few minutes earlier and was cruising along at 30 km/h. I wasn't comfortable going any faster. Not on that road. It was barely wide enough for two cars, and its sides were rimmed by bushes and a stone wall.

Perhaps I would have noticed the Porsche coming up behind me if I hadn't been on the phone to my wife. Philippa had stayed home, not being a fan of the friends I was meeting. That was a relief, because partners were not welcome tonight.

Once a year, Brendan, Rick and I met at a pub called The Night, located at the top of the mountain. We'd been doing it for eleven years, ever since we finished school. Our meet-up was always the first Saturday in October. Life had got so busy that we no longer met often during the rest of the year, what with work and family.

There was no question of driving home drunk, because the pub doubled as an inn. When we'd had our fill at the bar, we just made our way upstairs to the guest rooms. In the morning, we always had a big fried breakfast before leaving. As many eggs, rashers and slices of toast as we could handle. Philippa didn't understand the appeal. She thought Brendan was a loser and Rick was an arrogant bore.

We lived a twenty-minute drive away, and I'd kissed Philippa goodbye before I left. I wasn't expecting to talk to her again until the next day, but she rang me because she'd tried to buy a dress online and found that our joint account didn't have enough money in it.

"It must be a mistake," I said.

"No, Bill, I checked the balance."

I could hear the ice in her voice. She took financial matters very seriously. Never wasted a cent. I said, "I'll look into it tomorrow, okay?"

"Bill, have you been gambling again?"

"No."

"Don't lie to me. I've just logged in. I'm looking at the bank account right now. I can see the cash withdrawals. 600, 600, 600. You've been taking out as much cash as you can, every day this week."

No one knew I'd been going to The Night a lot lately, by myself. Casinos are illegal in Ireland. But private clubs are allowed to offer gambling services to members. One such private club, called The Luck of the Night, stood next to the pub, and I'd become a regular visitor lately. At the start, I made a little money. Putting it down to my skill, I became bold. As soon as I upped the stakes, my luck changed. Everything I did to try and work my way out only made things worse.

"Philippa, listen," I said.

Before I could say another word, the Porsche came out of nowhere. Blazing headlights in the rear-view mirror. Engine roar in my ears. The silver sportscar pulled up beside me, close enough to touch, and veered towards the Escort.

I jerked the wheel sideways and drove into a bush next to the road. For a terrifying moment, I felt the vehicle lose its stability. I thought I was going to hit the wall and roll. I jerked the wheel back the other way. The car levelled out on the road as I watched the Porsche zoom ahead.

"Bloody hell."

Philippa said, "What happened?"

I hit the brake. At the same time, I leaned on the horn as hard as I could. It was an almighty sound out there, in the middle of nowhere. The Porsche's brake lights came on. The sportscar came to a stop a short distance ahead, just before a twist in the road.

"Bill? What's happening?"

"Some cretin in a Porsche nearly ran me off the road."

"Are you okay?"

I eased to a stop as the Porsche reversed. It came to a halt six or seven metres in front of my bumper.

"Bill?" Philippa said.

I watched the door open, saw a huge guy get out of the car. He must have been six three, and almost as wide. Mid-forties, sandy hair. I don't know how he even managed to fit in the car. He looked like a wrestler. Despite the cold evening, he wore a thin shirt, with the sleeves rolled up above the elbow.

"Bill?"

"I need to go, Philippa. The guy is coming over here. He looks really angry."

"*He* looks angry? I thought he was the bad driver?"

"I know, right?"

But my own anger was starting to blend into anxiety.

"Don't let your temper get the better of you, Bill. Just stay in the car."

I was thinking the same thing myself. "Talk to you later."

I ended the call and dropped the phone in my lap as the guy came over to my window. He leaned down and eyeballed me.

"Open up," he mouthed.

I gave a shake of the head. I'd got pretty fat since the wedding and I was in no shape for a fight. Hell, the steering wheel was nearly resting on my belly.

The guy slammed his palm against the window. I was thinking I should get the car going. But then the guy moved away, towards his own car, and I breathed a sigh of relief, figuring that was the end of it.

With my shirtsleeve, I wiped the sheen of sweat off my face. When my eyes refocused, I saw the guy coming at me with a crowbar.

As soon as he got close, he swung at the windscreen. I covered my face as the glass cracked into a spiderweb pattern. He swung again. The crowbar hit the windscreen and shattered it even more.

"What's your problem?" I shouted.

He came around to the driver's window. He leaned down again, speaking loud enough for me to hear him through the glass. "Get out of the car. You owe me that."

"Are you nuts? I don't owe you a thing."

The guy brought back the crowbar, getting ready to swing again.

The windscreen was so badly cracked, I couldn't see a damn thing, but I hit the accelerator anyway.

I had a brief moment of relief before I smashed into the Porsche. The impact jolted me in my seat and there was a crunch of bumper on bumper.

Somewhere my phone started ringing. Philippa, no doubt, wanting to check in on me. The sound just distracted me.

Panicking now, I reversed fast. I wanted to get out of there. The Escort shot backwards. I looked in the mirror just as the man stepped in the car's path. There was a thump and he disappeared from view.

TWO

I hit the brake hard, causing my phone to slide off my lap onto the floor. Had I hit the guy? I didn't want to get out of the car, but I had to check if he was alright, if he needed an ambulance. I waited, staring in my rear-view mirror, hoping he'd show himself.

Surely I couldn't have killed him?

Moments earlier, my life had been okay. Sure, I was broke, and my gambling had grown bad again. My debts were out of control. But I'd have taken care of that. Philippa would have helped me figure out what to do. Now things were a million times worse.

Somewhere down at my feet, my phone stopped ringing, then started again.

Leave me alone, Philippa.

I braced myself and opened the door an inch.

I waited.

Nothing. No movement.

So I stepped outside.

The Porsche's engine was still running. Aside from the sound of the two cars, all was silent on the rolling hills around me.

In the space of a few seconds, dusk seemed to give way to night. It was almost fully dark. I walked around the side of the car. Slow, deliberate steps, making as little noise as possible.

I reached the back of the car. I expected to see the man lying dead on the road. As I came around the corner of the rear bumper, though, I saw nothing.

No sign of him.

Where the hell did he go?

The crunch of gravel behind me gave me my answer. I turned and ducked, just as he swung the crowbar at my face. I felt the breeze as it passed within an inch of my nose.

The guy must have sneaked all the way around the car to take me by surprise. I scrambled to the Escort and jumped in the passenger seat, because that was the closest door, while the guy came up behind. My heart was hammering like crazy. This was more nerve-shredding than any poker game I'd ever played. That was for use.

As I crawled across the gear stick, he grabbed my shoe. I kicked out, but the angle made it hard to get a decent blow in. When he tried to pull me out of the car, my shoe came away in his hand. He looked at it in disgust, then threw it over his shoulder.

I flipped onto my side and lashed out again, kicking him in the face as he came at me again.

I managed to get into the driver's seat. I hit the accelerator hard with my shoeless foot. The Escort shot forward.

I just about avoided hitting the Porsche again.

I couldn't see much through the windscreen, the passenger door was wide open, my shoe was gone, and I figured I was one more fright away from a heart attack. To cap it all off, the guy was chasing me down the road. And he was gaining.

I sped up. I kept going like that until I'd turned the corner. Then I stopped for a moment so that I could shut the passenger door. Then I got moving again, going slow because of the reduced visibility.

I knew I didn't have to go far.

The Night was just ahead.

I reached the pub after a couple of minutes. It was set into a big patch of land at the side of the road. The Night was a fat building, two storeys tall, painted white, with a thatched roof, like a traditional Irish cottage, but much bigger. Next to it was the private club, a small, modern-looking building with *The Luck of the Night* written in neon over its door.

The two buildings looked like they belonged to different times, different places. It was a weird juxtaposition, especially in the mountains, with fields around us.

There was enough parking for maybe three dozen cars. Tonight, the lot was half empty. I parked at the end of a row of cars and stepped outside. The gravel ground felt sharp through my socked foot.

I walked into the lounge. The place was made to look like you were in somebody's home circa 1974. It had old carpets in a variety of browns, old Guinness ads framed on the walls, a few record players and dozens of vinyl LPs strewn about on shelves.

I pushed through the crowd until I caught sight of Brendan and Rick sitting in a nook. It had a rounded leather couch in a U shape, around a table, perfect for the three of us. They were just finishing their pints.

Brendan moved his jacket, which he'd used to reserve the third seat. His hairline had receded an inch since I'd last seen him a few months earlier and his face was ham-pink in the sickly pub light.

"Alright?" Brendan said.

Beside him, Rick looked as dapper as ever in a crisp shirt and designer jeans. He'd got some new thick-rimmed glasses since the last time I saw him. A newspaper sat on the table next to his drink.

"What happened to you?" Rick said.

My hands and legs were shaking from the experience I'd just had. I slumped in the couch. While I was gathering my thoughts, a barmaid came by and Rick ordered a round.

"You're not going to believe it," I said once she'd gone. I told them what had happened.

"Piss off," Rick said.

I held up my foot, the one with no shoe, as evidence.

"You need to report that," he said.

"I will. I just need a minute to recover."

The drinks came and I knocked back half my beer in one long gulp.

"Better?" Rick asked. A wry smile passed over his face.

"Yeah."

And I was, until the driver of the Porsche walked in.

THREE

The Porsche guy looked just as large inside the pub as he had on the road. Even larger, because now he was towering over the other punters. His shirt was stretched tight over his huge chest. He looked all around, like he was searching for someone. I sank down low in my seat and hoped he wouldn't see me.

"What are you doing?" Brendan said.

"That's him."

Brendan and Rick followed my gaze.

"He doesn't look so tough," Brendan said.

Rick snorted and said, "I know that guy."

"Who is he?" I hissed.

"He's the owner. Don't you ever read the news?"

"The owner of what?"

"Of this place," Rick said impatiently.

Sure enough, when the man got to the bar, he didn't order a drink, but slipped behind the counter and disappeared into a back room. He was carrying something long and thin in his hand.

I don't know why but the idea that he owned this place struck terror into me. Perhaps it was the thought that I was on his turf.

I sat up in my seat.

"Does he own the club next door too?"

Rick nodded. "Same owner."

"What's his name?"

"Dale Winters. He's into all that mixed martial arts shit. Trying to make a name for himself."

No wonder he was so eager for a fight. But I wondered what made him drive like a maniac in the first place.

"Guys, I've lost a lot of money in that club."

I hadn't intended to say that, but I had to get it out.

Both of my friends looked at me aghast.

"What? When?" Rick said. "How much?"

I shrugged, trying to look casual. "The last few weeks. I'm actually down a few grand. They've started phoning me about it."

"Well done, Bill," Rick said. "How many thousand do you owe?"

"Um, about seven."

Brendan puffed up his chest. "You know, that place is rigged."

"Shut up," Rick said. "How do you know?"

"That's what I've heard."

"It's not rigged," Brendan said. "Bill here is just throwing his money away."

I took a fortifying gulp of beer, then got to my feet.

"I'm going to go and write down the Porsche's license plate number."

Brendan nodded his approval. "Finally a good idea."

I hurried across the pub floor and outside. It was fully dark now. The lighting in the car park was non-existent, so I moved through a ghostly world of dark shapes. At least the Porsche was easily recognisable by shape.

I found the back of the car and waited for my eyes to adjust. There was no license plate. The bumper had been badly damaged – by me, I supposed – and the license plate must have fallen off. Perhaps that was what Dale Winters had been carrying when he entered the bar.

I went around the front of the car and tried to read the plate there, but it was covered in mud and, through the darkness, I couldn't make it out. In any case, I realised that I didn't have anything to write the number down on, or even a pen to write with.

I felt in my pocket for my phone, but it wasn't there. I remembered it sliding off my lap when I was driving, remembered it lying on the floor, ringing. I'd forgotten to pick it up.

I walked across the car park, heading to the Escort. I reached the space where I'd left the car.

It was empty.

I stared at the place where my car should have been. I was sure this was where I had left it. Even though the car park was dark, I knew. I'd left the car at the very end of a row. It had only been ten minutes earlier.

Someone stole my car.

It was the only explanation I could think of. And there was only one person who'd do such a thing.

Dale Winters must have noticed it there, and towed it. Maybe he had a truck parked around the back of the buildings.

I walked back to the Porsche.

"Jerk," I shouted and kicked the side of his car.

I jumped up onto the bonnet. Once I'd found my balance, I set about kicking the windscreen in, using my one shoe. It was harder work than I thought, but after a while the windscreen cracked. The car's alarm began to blare.

Startled, I dropped to the ground, just as the door to the pub opened. It was him. Dale Winters. He was lit up in the doorway for a second before he disappeared into the darkness, moving towards me.

I hunkered down and crawled around the back of the Porsche as Dale Winters reached it. He turned off the alarm. There was silence for a moment. Then he exploded in a fit of bad language. I guess he'd noticed my tap-dance on his windscreen.

"Hey, Bill," he shouted. "Are you out there? You're going to pay for this."

I felt like my blood dropped thirty degrees in one second. How the hell did he know my name? Sure, I'd been in the club and the pub he owned, but before today I'd never seen him.

Dale started walking back across the car park to the pub. He pulled out his phone as he walked, dialling a number and putting the phone to his ear as he disappeared back inside.

Seeing what the owner was like, I could well believe that the club cheated its members, as Brendan had suggested. Maybe that was why I'd had such bad luck.

I didn't want to go straight into the lounge after Dale had. I didn't want him to see me. So I decided to look for the Escort. I skirted around the side of the pub. There was an employee-only area there, but it was blocked by a tall wall with razor wire on top. I tried the gate and found it locked. I was sure that bastard had towed my car in there. I couldn't get at it, though.

I stood there, feeling a deflated. Then I thought of Philippa. I'd have to call her. She must be worried about me. I could borrow Brendan or Rick's phone, but what was Philippa's number? I had no idea. I relied on my phone to remember that kind of thing. Maybe I could e-mail her instead.

I re-traced my steps and entered the lounge. There was no sign of Dale Winters, so I hurried back to the table. Three fresh beers sat there.

"What happened?" Brendan asked.

I said, "Grab your drinks, lads. We're changing location."

FOUR

Brendan and Rick grumbled. They thought I was making a big deal out of very little, but they reluctantly agreed to follow me upstairs. Rick had already collected the keys to our rooms. They were actual keys, chunky pieces of metal, rather than cards. It was that kind of place. The three of us assembled, pints in hand, in my room. It was near the back of the building. We barely fitted inside. There was only one chair, which Rick insisted on taking. He set down his glass and his newspaper on the tiny bedside unit. Brendan and I sat next to each other on the bed.

"Do you know how to hotwire a car?" I said to Brendan. If any of us would know, it was him.

He looked a little insulted and said, "I haven't done that for years. Why?"

"That bastard took mine." I filled them in briefly, then told them what I was thinking. "He stole the Escort, so I want to take his Porsche."

"Are you crazy?" Rick slapped his beer down on the bedside unit. "Don't escalate this thing."

"Dale Winters cheated me at the club and now he's stolen my car. Not to mention that he nearly killed me."

Rick had nothing to say to that.

He took a sip of beer and stroked his chin thoughtfully.

I was too impatient to sit still. I walked to the window. It looked out onto a storage area. A line of kegs stood against the wall at the side of the yard. I guess this was where deliveries came in, where supplies were loaded into the pub.

I was sure it was also where my car had been taken. There were a couple of cars parked around, but it was so dark, I couldn't tell if one of them was mine.

I lifted the window. Outside, the roof of a one-storey annex was just below my window. It sloped downwards towards the back yard a few metres away. I figured I could walk to the edge, then drop down to the ground without killing myself. I scrambled through the window, ignoring my friends' protests. A terrible desire for revenge had gripped me and I couldn't resist. I released my grip on the windowsill and walked down the roof, doing my best to stay balanced. My one shoe was a hindrance rather than a help, so I slipped it off. My grip was better when I was just wearing socks.

Rick hissed at me, "Get back in here, Bill. You're going to kill yourself."

Ignoring him, I took another step.

"What are you going to do?" Brendan asked.

"Stop distracting me."

"Come on, Bill, get back in here!"

There was a screech of steel below me.

I whispered, "Guys, shut up. Someone's coming."

There were footsteps. Two men stepped outside. I could tell right away that one of them was Winters. Even from above, the guy looked huge.

"Check every room," Winters said. "Find that prick. He's here somewhere."

"You got it," the second man said in a low voice.

My breath caught in my throat. They could only be talking about me. Our personal vendetta was getting more intense by the minute. Well, I was sick of being pushed around – by Philippa, by my friends, by my urge to gamble. My fight with Winters was one thing I wasn't going to lose. I'd beat him if it killed me.

I heard the clang of the steel door as it slammed shut. Winters was standing outside alone now. A trail of smoke rose from his cigarette. I glanced back. Brendan and Rick were still pressed together at the window. Thankfully they both kept silent. Rick beckoned me to come inside. I shook my head.

Instead, I moved closer to the edge of the roof. Winters had his back to me. I was about to lower myself onto my belly when I lost balance.

My right foot slid out from under me.

The world flipped.

My back slammed into the roof, and I rolled down the slope and over the edge.

Winters spun around and caught sight of me as I tumbled down at him. It was a fall of about ten feet and I smashed right into him. He cushioned my fall a little, though it was still a rough landing. My elbow hit the ground and searing pain exploded down my arm. Winters fared worse though, as most of my weight hit his chest. The impact winded him completely and his head smashed back against the ground.

I staggered to my feet, feeling ridiculous in my socks. Winters wore shiny black shoes with pointed toes. The disparity made me feel vulnerable.

When Winters tried to sit up, I didn't hesitate to give him a smack in the face. He groaned but I remembered that he was a martial arts expert as well as a nutjob. If the two of us had a straight fight, I'd end up in a casket. So I gave him a hard kick and looked around, wondering how the hell I could get out of there. The gate was still locked. But the doorway to the pub probably wasn't.

I ran over to it and tried it. Sure enough, the door opened with a screech of metal.

I ran in and locked it behind me. There was a narrow corridor, which I followed, emerging in a kitchen with half a dozen staff members milling around. This was where all those fried breakfasts I'd eaten over the years had been prepared. It was hard now not to think of them all being tainted by Dale Winters. I imagined him walking through here with his henchman, a cigarette in his hand.

Ignoring the staff, I hurried out the other side of the kitchen, emerging in the back of the lounge. The table where I'd met Brendan and Rick a short time earlier was now occupied by three ladies. I hurried to the stairwell at the side of the lounge. Without a car, there was nowhere to go but back to my room so I hurried up the narrow staircase.

In the upstairs corridor I nearly walked straight into a thin, rat-faced man. He looked at me, then looked down at my feet. It was him. The guy Winters had been speaking to. Standing there in his leather jacket, with his little goatee, he looked exactly like some kind of small-time criminal.

He came at me. Maybe to grab me, maybe to bustle past me and tell his boss. Either way, I wasn't having it.

I pushed him. He pushed me back. Then I slammed him back into the wall, and he let out a loud grunt. The door to my room opened and Brendan looked out.

"Grab him," I said.

"Huh?"

Now Rick stood in the doorway too. The thug was recovering, and my friends were standing there like a couple of dipsticks. It seemed I had to do everything myself.

I grabbed the guy and dragged him into the room. Brendan and Rick stepped back to let me in but made no effort to help. I flung the guy down on the floor and slammed the door.

"What are you doing?" Rick said.

"Winters and this guy are up to something. Planning to kill me, maybe."

The rat-faced man tried to get to his feet.

I said, "Stay down, asshole."

He didn't so I gave him a kick that made him.

Brendan stared at me. He said, "Bill? Do you want to face a charge of false imprisonment?"

I laughed bitterly. "I don't think Winters wants the law sniffing around his business. Right?" I hunkered down in front of the thug. He was sitting on his backside looking like he wanted to kill me. "Where's my car?"

"Your car? What car?"

I slapped him across the face. "Remember now?"

He growled, "Mr. Winters wants to talk to you. You're making a serious mistake."

"Not as serious as the one your boss made when he nearly killed me."

The guy flashed me an ugly smile. "He's having a bad day."

"What kind of day do you think I'm having?"

Rick raised his hands. "Let's everyone calm the fuck down. Now, Bill, I'm not having anything to do with this shit."

"Me neither," Brendan said. "Come on. Let's get out of here. You can come back for your car later."

"No way."

Rick snorted. "Suit yourself, but I'm not sticking around."

He walked out of the room.

Brendan gave an apologetic shrug. "Rick's right. Come on, let's get out of here."

He grabbed my arm, but I shrugged it off. "I'm not going anywhere."

"Fine. Have it your way."

With a shrug, Brendan walked out. I was alone with Winters's man. He got to his feet, no longer intimidated by three men, instead only facing one very out-of-shape one.

He said, "I told you, you're making a big mistake. You owe us."

"What do you mean?"

"The club." He smiled. "You lost a lot at poker. A lot at blackjack too."

I'd never seen this man before, but he must have been watching me at The Luck of the Night, maybe over CCTV. He didn't look like a security guard. Not a very high-class one anyway, given the gangster vibe. But the club wasn't very high class either. If it was, I'd never have been allowed in.

"My gambling is none of your business," I said, trying to hide how shaken I felt.

"Mr. Winters? He'll keep your car. But he wants more than that now. It would have been easier if you didn't make him mad."

Was that why he nearly ran me off the road? Had he noticed me approaching his club, where I was already underwater with debt, and made a business decision to demand the keys to my car? Had he wanted it even back then? He'd never got around to explanations because of the way things deteriorated.

The man took a menacing step towards me.

"Stay back," I warned. I looked around for some weapon but there was nothing. All I could see was Brendan's newspaper. I grabbed it, rolled it up and jabbed it at the thug. "Stay back."

He didn't look intimidated and my confidence was diminishing by the second.

I backed out of the room, pulled the door shut behind me and hurried downstairs and out the door of the lounge. Brendan and Rick's shadowy forms were moving to the left. I headed the other way, to the Porsche. If I couldn't take it for myself, I decided Dale couldn't have it either. I took my cigarette lighter out of my pocket and set fire to Brendan's newspaper, then jumped up on the Porsche's bonnet. I gave the cracked windscreen a few more kicks, until a hole formed, then stuffed the burning paper through the gap.

I jumped down and waited a moment, but nothing happened. Maybe the fire had gone out already?

Nothing was going my way today.

And what was I going to do now?

I had to get out of there.

I set off across the car park towards Brendan and Rick. As I did so, a car pulled into the lot. The driver came to a stop in front of the door to the lounge. Just then, the door to the pub opened. Out came Dale Winters and his right-hand man.

A lady stepped out of the car. Philippa? Yes, it was her. My wife walked over to the two men. I felt pure terror then. Not for myself, but for her, seeing her so close to those brutes. She had no idea who she was dealing with.

Philippa handed something to Winters. I broke into a sprint, my belly bouncing up and down.

"Get away from her," I shouted.

The three of them turned and squinted into the darkness. Winters smiled when he saw me, then turned to Philippa. Was he going to hurt her? Take out his rage on my wife instead of me? As I approached, Winters held out his hand.

I called to her, "Get away from him, Philippa."

Instead she took Winters's hand in hers and shook it.

"What are you doing?" I said as I reached her.

Her face was like stone.

"Saving your hide, Bill."

FIVE

Winters held up the cheque and examined it. With the way the overhead light fell on his features, the man looked like the devil.

He said, “Alright. We’re square, Bill. Now fuck off before I change my mind.”

“Hold on. What? How?” I turned to Philippa. “We have no money.”

“It’s the college fund.”

Her voice was quiet but firm. The college fund was her pet project. We didn’t even have kids yet, but for years she’d been setting money aside for our future children. I’d actually forgotten about that account. If I’d remembered, I might have gambled that money away too.

“You treat that lady right,” Winters said. “She’s a good one.”

“Shut up, Winters. Philippa, you paid off my debts?”

“It’s the last time,” Philippa said. “Mr. Winters called me soon after you and I were speaking on the phone. He told me how serious things had got. Said he was going to bleed the money out of you. I couldn't let that happen."

"That's why she added fifty percent," Winters said with a smile. "After all, I'll have to get a new windscreen for the Porsche."

I could have cried, I was so overwhelmed with gratitude. I knew how lucky I was. And I knew how much that college fund meant to Philippa.

"I'll never be so reckless again," I promised. "I'll fill up that college fund for our little ones."

"You better."

We hugged. Our special moment was broken by Winters laying his heavy mitt on my shoulder.

He said, "You're barred from the pub and you're barred from the club. I ever see you again, I ever have any reason to hear your name again, you're dead. Got that?"

"Get your hand off me," I said.

I had no intention of ever returning to the pub, and my desire to gamble had just withered up inside me.

"Come on," Philippa said.

She got behind the wheel of her car. I took a last look at the two gangsters. Then I got in the passenger seat. Winters and his sidekick watched as we moved slowly away. Philippa drove like a snail but I wasn't going to complain. Her prudence had saved me.

"Thank you," I said. "Really."

She sighed.

"I know you, Bill. You'd have ended up in some kind of awful tit-for-tat with that man until one of you got hurt."

I was too ashamed to admit it, but she was probably right. In the moment, all I'd wanted was bloody revenge.

"I still love you," she said.

Then I really did cry. Blinking quickly, I watched as Philippa carefully looked both ways and pulled out onto the road.

"I can't wait to get home," I said.

I was exhausted after all that had happened. And I felt a bit bruised and sore. I flipped down the mirror to see how I looked. I'd taken a few tumbles during the evening and wondered how my face had fared.

What caught my attention in the mirror was not my face, though. It was the flames behind us. I twisted in my seat and looked back at the car park.

"Oh god," I groaned.

"Bill, what is it?"

"Oh no."

"You're scaring me."

In the car park behind us, Winters's Porsche had turned into an inferno. It was that stupid newspaper I set on fire. I'd forgotten about it after Philippa arrived. I thought the flame got gone out.

Figures gathered around the burning car. They were just silhouettes against the background of flame. But one of them was huge. And he looked mad. Even at this distance, I could tell that from his posture.

Winters would come after me. Him and his man. They'd come to our house.

Suddenly my horror turned into a kind of giddy delight. The house was my turf and if they attacked me there I'd have the home advantage. I felt a perverse frisson of excitement as I started to think about how I could ambush them. I'd get them back for what they'd done.

"Bill? What is it?"

Philippa's eyes were wide. Her voice trembled.

I decided I'd pack her off to her friend's house and then do what I needed to do. By morning I'd have got rid of the bodies. She'd never know a thing. It would be perfect.

"Nothing," I said, patting Philippa's leg. "Everything's going to be okay."

Printed in Great Britain
by Amazon

35755442R00094